HEATHER BOYD

Almost an Equal

HUNT CLUB – 1

DEDICATION

This book is dedicated to my mentor, Jordan. Thank you for your inspiration, ideas and dedication to sharing your knowledge with so many others.

BY HEATHER BOYD

ALMOST AN EQUAL
BARELY A MASTER
HARDLY A STRANGER

JUST A DREAM
NEVER A GENTLEMAN
ONCE A HUSBAND

CHAPTER ONE

April, 1814

Nathan Stern, Duke of Byworth, glanced at the pale note on his dark desk, anger burning through his usually contained demeanor. No one threatened a duke and got away with the impertinence. But in this case his hands might be tied.

The note from the Duke of Lewes threatening to publish Nathan's wife's diary could prove . . . uncomfortable.

How uncomfortable would depend on what exactly his duchess had written about their estranged marriage. If she'd written even part of the truth—he would hang.

A chair creaked in the adjoining small chamber.

He turned his head and caught his steward glancing swiftly back down at his papers. Nathan took a deep breath and buried his apprehension. He could not disclose his fears to his most trusted employee because if he did he'd no longer have him close by.

Although his thoughts were improper, and any action taken to fulfill them life threatening, he let his gaze rest on what he could see of the other man. Tall, neat and as sleek as a cat, Mr. Henry Stackpool had drawn his eye from the moment their paths had crossed. Stackpool's interview for the position of steward had gone badly, but not because of anything he had done. It had been Nathan who struggled not to grin like a fool and then covered it with excessive coughing. His gaze had drifted over the lanky younger man and dreamed . . . of things that should not be.

A familiar ache pinched his chest. Unfortunately, the

other man did not share Nathan's inclinations. He was proper down to his highly polished toes.

Nathan folded the paper and slipped it under his desk blotter. He'd deal with the Lewes problem later when he had time to form an appropriate response and course of action. But for now he had estate business to take care of.

He stood and crossed to the adjoining room. "Have you finished those letters, Stackpool?"

The younger man collected a short stack of papers and held them out. "I am almost finished, Your Grace. However, there is one request that requires further investigation before I draft a reply. If you have pressing business elsewhere I can leave it on your desk for your signature either tonight or tomorrow morning."

If Stackpool needed more time, then he needed it. No amount of grumbling on Nathan's part or hovering would get the job done any faster. Yet, he stalled for time, rifling through the close written sheets and drinking in the warmth of Stackpool's tiny office. At times he wished there might be a second chair installed beside the desk so he might sit and simply spend time with his steward. To converse as friends. But he had no idea how to bridge the gap that society dictated must exist between a man of his rank and a mere servant, nor did he know if he should even try. He valued Stackpool for his diligence and for his honesty, and he couldn't risk losing his good regard.

Besides, he couldn't linger. He had a vital mission to undertake upstairs in a few moments. His children had demanded he visit them earlier than usual today and would be cross if he became distracted. He'd thought it was a secret between them, but Nathan should have guessed Stackpool would have learned already.

Nathan folded his arms across his chest. "I see news travels fast."

A small smile tightened Stackpool's mouth, his eyes betrayed his amusement. He glanced away before Nathan could return the smile. "I've no idea to what you refer,

Your Grace."

Nathan wished he could speak with Stackpool as an equal, but the man would be horrified if he discovered how equal he wished to become. He glanced at the sheets in his hands again. "I'll deal with these in the morning too, along with your last piece of correspondence. Now, I should probably get along to the nursery."

Another gentle smile quirked Stackpool's lips, and Nathan, fearing the temptation, turned away abruptly. He returned to his desk, dropped the papers on the shiny surface and hurried out his door before he did something foolish.

After climbing the endless flights of stairs he approached the nursery door quietly. He pressed his ear against the wood and listened. Inside, his children were arguing.

"No, I get to sit next to Papa."

"Mama said he's too busy to come."

"He'll come. Mr. Stackpool promised to remind him."

A grin tugged Nathan's lips. Stackpool would never let him forget a promise to his children. His steward had, from time to time, mentioned his children in passing, prompting Nathan to remember them even when his burdens grew overwhelming. That was why he couldn't bear to lose Stackpool. He wanted to be a better, more involved father than his own had been. But he occassionally needed to be reminded.

He eased the door open and slipped inside.

His children shrieked with pleasure and he covered his ears as they swamped him.

"You're early," his five year old daughter, Cecily, accused, fists settling on her hips in a near-perfect imitation of her mother's haughty manner.

Nathan sighed and bent low to press a kiss to her cheek, hoping she'd grow out it sooner than later. "I finished early today."

Unlike her mother, Cecily smiled and clapped her hands together. "Wonderful. Will Mr. Stackpool be joining us too? He promised to help me with my project."

He set his hand to her cheek. "Stackpool has pressing matters to attend to. I'm sure he will visit later if he can. Now, what entertainments have you planned for our evening?"

Although his daughter pouted, she hurried across the room.

"Good evening, Father."

Nathan gazed at his eldest son. Although it seemed impossible, James appeared taller than he was yesterday. Any day now, he expected to turn around and find a young man not an eleven-year-old. "How are you today, my boy?"

"Very well, thank you. And you?"

"My health is excellent."

James nodded and glanced away. Although Nathan hadn't intended for this awkwardness, a chasm had opened up between him and his eldest son. He found it difficult to bridge the growing distance as it reminded him of his own interactions with his father.

Nathan had envisaged a different life for his son than the indifferent upbringing he'd experienced. Yet he had no idea how to obtain it. He followed James' gaze to where it rested on his middle child. Pierce, at seven, was the most bookish of all his children. He lived with his head perpetually bent over his papers, a worried frown or scowl gifted on the words before him, and not on his newly arrived father.

James cleared his throat, attempting to gain his brother's attention.

Pierce didn't look up.

When James seemed about to cross the room, Nathan set his hand to his son's shoulder to still him. "It's all right. Go back to your amusements."

With a final scowl, James turned away, leaving Nathan to approach his other son.

He caught up a chair and placed it directly before the boy, then leaned forward and placed his finger on the top of his page.

Pierce blinked, gaze rising to Nathan's finger and then to his face. "Oh, Father, I never heard you come in. Do you know it says here that the Blue Spotted Wren is only found in Dorset? Quite remarkable."

Nathan suppressed a smile. "Really. How fascinating."

Like the obedient child he was, Pierce carefully marked his place in the book and set it aside. He glanced around Nathan's shoulder. "Did Mr. Stackpool not come with you today? I had some questions for him."

Nathan ruffled Pierce's hair, satisfied they were coming to view Stackpool as a favorite servant. "As I told your sister when I first came in, Stackpool has other business."

The boy nodded. "It can wait until tomorrow morning."

"What happens tomorrow morning?"

His son's face flushed with color and Pierce hastily glanced at his siblings. He pressed his lips together and didn't speak.

James moved nearer Cecily and set his hands over her shoulders.

Nathan scowled. "Children, answer me. You know I don't like secrets. What happens tomorrow morning?"

James pushed his sister behind him as Pierce scampered to hide too.

"Mr. Stackpool visits us each morning," James declared, appearing ready for a confrontation over the matter.

Nathan took in the boy's posturing and smiled. "And why would you think I'd dislike the notion? Mr. Stackpool is a sensible conversationalist."

James licked his lips. "Well, we figured that if we had to keep it a secret from Mama then we shouldn't tell you."

"Oh." Nathan did his best to keep his voice neutral. What the devil had Stackpool been doing with his children? He was aware that Stackpool had been pressed to read to them each night, but to visit them in the morning too?

"It's just that . . . if we tell, you'll make us stand up and do it. It would be beyond mortifying to do it in front of Mama's friends."

Nathan sank into a chair. "What is Mr. Stackpool teaching you?"

James blushed and looked away, then mumbled, "To dance."

For a moment, Nathan thought he'd misheard. There was no need to keep dancing a secret. Their mother loved to dance and constantly berated him for not securing a dance instructor so she might show her children off to her friends. He frowned as he took in his children's distraught faces.

By the way they fidgeted, he guessed they didn't care for the notion of dancing for their mother like trained monkeys. And he couldn't blame them.

He held out his hand to Cecily and she came forward to perch on his knee. "I have no objections to the lessons or keeping them secret."

James' stiff posture softened. "Well, we know we must learn to dance, and Cecily enjoys dancing with Stackpool, but . . . I shouldn't care to let anyone see us dance together."

Nathan nodded solemnly, fighting to contain his relief that their big secret proved inconsequential. "I can see where that might become uncomfortable. But I must say you've all done a marvelous job of hiding your activities."

James let out a breath. "Well, our lessons are held early while mama still sleeps."

Nathan clapped his hand against his son's shoulder, the gesture again reminding him of the awkward moments of affection his father had bestowed. If only James could unbend a little like his brother Pierce. "I had no idea Mr. Stackpool excelled at the art. You must tell me how early you attend to your lessons so I may see your progress."

"We meet at six."

He winced. "In the morning?"

All the children nodded quickly.

"For goodness sake, couldn't you let the man sleep until a decent hour? With you three demanding his time at all hours it surprises me that he hasn't fallen asleep at his desk."

Poor bloody Stackpool. The man was a saint. Given Nathan's occasional need to keep him working until the wee hours of the morning, he'd not shown an ounce of fatigue to hint that he was being cruelly taken advantage of. Nathan would have to curtail these impromptu lessons or lower his own demands for Stackpool's time. If he didn't, Stackpool would leave him for better conditions and a better night's sleep and Nathan didn't much care for that idea at all.

CHAPTER TWO

Henry Stackpool listened for noise in the hall again and then lifted the Duke of Byworth's desk blotter.

Beneath lay the paper his employer had taken from him before he'd had a chance to read the missive properly. All he knew was that the Duke of Lewes had written but precious little beyond. However, the note had unsettled Byworth. Henry could never remember him being so tense.

With a last glance at the closed door, Henry picked it up and flipped it open.

I have your wife's diary. Come Friday to discuss terms. You know where. Lewes.

Relief coursed through Henry followed by concern. Although the matter didn't affect him directly, he did fear for His Grace. Lewes, a man he knew better than he wished, could be ruthless. He would make Byworth pay high for the return of his own property.

Henry slipped the note back in place, and then laid his completed correspondence on the blotter to await the duke's attention. He blew out the duke's candles and closed the door to the study before extinguishing his own lights and pondered the diary's potential contents.

Given the duke's distraction since receiving that note, Henry feared the diary contained damaging gossip about his generous employer. A man who, despite the inconsistencies in Henry's application, had offered him the position of steward and turned his life around for the better.

Henry glanced around his office with pride. There were days when he couldn't believe his good fortune in securing this position and he did everything in his power to do his job well, even if it meant losing some of his free time to the duke's children. At least they appreciated his attention.

Henry closed and locked his office then hurried for the servant's stairs. A blast of heat swept his face as he reached the lower landing and he looked up as he entered the kitchen.

"Ah, there ya are, Mr. Stackpool. I'd feared you'd fallen asleep over your work."

He smiled at the cook. "No chance of that, Mrs. Mayberry. The duke is hardly a hard taskmaster, but there is much to be done."

The older lady snorted. "If you ask me the duke is as soft as butter on the inside."

Henry thought that might be true. He'd never met a man before who commanded with merely a glance and a softly worded request. Henry's concerns over the duke's letter surfaced as he sank to the hard wood bench. Whatever happened, Lewes would exploit the contents of the diary for his own gain. Byworth simply had to get the duchess' property back before any damage could be done.

A plate landed before Henry and the cook sat with a groan. "It shouldn't be too bad." As Henry took his first mouthful, Mrs. Mayberry leaned forward. "Her Grace is in a right snit this evening. Be mindful not to cross her path."

He chewed quickly, striving to keep his disgust for his employer's wife buried deep. "Any idea what set her off this time?"

The duchess was the type of female who used the power of her title to get her way. She had, by Henry's count, dismissed six maids for supposedly slovenly habits, two grooms for attempting to impose on her person, and three footmen for rank stupidity. And she'd had her eye on him too. He knew why she disliked him. He wouldn't fall prey to her lascivious smiles. He wouldn't ever visit her bed.

"Well, the duke—he went to see her tonight. She's been ever so grouchy since then."

Conversations between the duke and duchess always seemed fraught with danger for the servants. The last time one of the maids earned a slap from the duchess for nothing at all.

"Thank you for the warning."

Henry shoveled another spoonful of stew into his mouth. How long could the biggest thorn in his side be avoided? The duchess made no bones about her displeasure that the duke kept him on despite her groundless accusations of impertinence. If not for the duke, and the pleasure of working for him, Henry would seek other employment and bide his time until he could be his own master.

The desire for freedom made him shift restlessly in his seat.

Cook, misinterpreting his mood, laughed. "Be off with you, lad. You've left your ladybird waiting long enough tonight."

He had no ladybird waiting in the village, but he let everyone think so, even if he kept closed-mouth about her identity. Henry pasted a smile on his face as he pushed his plate away. "That I have. Goodnight, Mayberry."

She winked. "Goodnight, sir. Be sure to be back early enough in the morning so no one notices."

Although he chuckled as he stepped out into the night air readily enough, his smile fell at the thought of the long, cold night ahead. But he had to keep up the pretense of an ordinary man—one with ordinary desires no one thought twice about him satisfying.

Henry hadn't been satisfied in a long time. That he'd

once been a whore to powerful men in London's Hunt Club was a secret he'd take to the grave. He still craved fleeting affection and the pleasure of touching another man who held similar desires. But he was always conscious that he couldn't trust anyone. Not if he wanted to keep his new life here, at any rate.

Henry hurried down Grantley Park's long driveway, while noting the moon peeking low on the horizon as the sun set on another exhausting day. Habits of his misspent youth were hard to break so he walked quickly on the grass to muffle his steps as he headed toward the village. About halfway down the drive he turned and glanced about. When he saw no one following from the Park, he took a step into the protection of the woods, angling toward a distant ruin.

A giggle to his right stilled him. Then another had him backing away.

Of all the rotten luck. Someone had secured a bower beneath the trees and appropriated the space for a seduction.

Reconciled to another costly night in the village, he continued on toward town, assured of falling asleep over a tankard at The Angel instead of his hard stone ledge. Weariness tugged at his limbs as the tavern lights came into view. These long days spent in the duke's employ were more demanding than his busiest Hunt Club day.

As he stepped across the tavern threshold a raucous laugh drew his attention. He stared into the Duke of Lewes' dark eyes and his heart leapt in fear. For a moment Henry considered escape. Then he forced his steps toward a far table, keeping his chin tucked low.

When the innkeeper deposited a tankard before him, he looked up with surprise. Lewes stood over his table.

"You seem familiar."

Henry stood quickly and touched his forelock. "Can I help you, my lord?"

"Your Grace," Lewes corrected.

"Beg pardon, Your Grace," Henry stammered. "I didn't recognize you."

Lewes pursed his lips as he studied Henry. While the duke looked his fill, Henry tried not to fidget. He hoped the duke had forgotten him enough not to make the connection to his time at the Hunt Club.

Lewes turned. "Innkeeper, a bottle of wine for my carriage."

Henry let out the breath he'd held.

"Come along, Arrow, no need to be coy. I've got a soft spot for you."

Henry gulped. *Hell.*

Given what he knew of Lewes, he had no choice but to go along with the duke or risk exposure for perversion. Although society considered Lewes a ladies man, what wasn't widely known was that he dabbled in trousers. He was a man of many and varied tastes, all of them quite painful.

As he followed Lewes outside, Henry glanced about. The moon had grown fuller with the passage into night, but a shiver shook him. When crossed, Lewes could be vicious with his fists. He had grievously wounded a friend of Henry's once.

Henry climbed into the carriage and, as it lurched forward, the duke dragged him into his lap. Lewes grabbed his hair and tugged. "You and Archer left London."

Henry winced. "Yes, Your Grace. I went into service."

The duke relaxed his grip, allowing Henry to scamper away. "And Archer?"

He shook his head. "I don't know where he went."

Lewes struck him, knocking his head hard against the squabs. Henry cursed.

The duke leaned forward to squeeze Henry's throat. "You'll tell me."

Henry wrapped both hands around Lewes' wrist and dug his fingers in. The duke gasped and relaxed his grip enough so Henry could breathe. His eyes glazed with desire. He was the sort of gent who enjoyed pain but, unlike some of his class, he preferred to be the recipient except when thwarted. Archer had known how far to push Lewes. Which most likely was why the duke appeared incensed his favorite entertainment had disappeared into thin air.

"If you don't deliver Archer up to me, you'll do my bidding in his place."

Even years after living outside the Hunt Club, the thought of those types of pleasures terrified his nights. He couldn't go back to that again. Summoning up bravado he didn't feel, Henry scowled. "I left that life behind."

"The only behind in your future is mine."

Henry crossed his arms over his chest, feigning boredom, ignoring the fact that Lewes still held his throat. "You cannot make me fuck you. I refuse."

Lewes flexed his fingers. The impatient gesture warned Henry to tread carefully. Given what Henry knew of the Duke of Lewes, he may have passed the point of being reasonable. If Henry didn't accede to the man's wishes, he'd loosen his frustration through violence.

Lewes sat back, his expression dark and frightening. "If you won't tell me what I need to know, if you refuse me, I will pass you over to men who'll make you like being their boy."

CHAPTER THREE

If there ever was a day when Nathan needed to see a friendly face then that day had surely come. For starters, he'd been woken late by the shrill whining of his wife demanding another rise in her quarterly allowance. Given that Nathan had been fast asleep, dreaming of frolicking with Stackpool amid the old ruin, he was less than happy with the interruption.

Then his children had arrived, disappointed that Stackpool had forgotten their early morning lesson and frustrated by their inability to find him. Nathan had shooed them away, but only after promising to send him a whole hour earlier that afternoon, even if Stackpool hadn't finished his duties.

But those duties had never been started today because Stackpool hadn't come. He glanced over at his steward's unoccupied chamber and heaved a heavy sigh. Given his meticulous attention to duty, Nathan was worried. It was not like him to be late or absent from the manor without sending word, and it now approached eleven. When Mr. Stackpool arrived, he would have some explaining to do.

A knock sounded at the door. "Come," he called, hoping to see Stackpool on the other side. Yet when his butler rounded the solid wood door, his heart fell to his boots.

"I've made considerable inquiries, Your Grace, and as near as I can tell Mr. Stackpool has not been seen since he dined last evening. According to Cook, he went out."

Nathan paced. "Out where?"

The butler grimaced. "I am led to believe he left to

meet with a sweetheart in the village."

He stopped as his chest squeezed painfully and then resumed pacing. Despite his disappointment, he should have accepted the signs. Many a man appeared attractive to him, yet not all matched his inclinations. Like most, Stackpool had his mind set on the safest path. Nathan should be happy he'd be spared a life of discontent.

The butler cleared his throat. "I imagine Mr. Stackpool will return soon. He's left his possessions behind."

Hope soared in Nathan's breast and he did his best to hide his relief. Even if he could never have him the way he wanted, at least he'd not be deprived of Stackpool's services and expertise. Already the stress of his burdens seemed heavier without Stackpool's steadying presence. "Thank you, Peters. You may go."

He turned for his desk and sat, and as soon as Peters closed the door, he slipped out the note from Lewes and read it. Come Friday. Like hell he would. He would visit tonight and catch Lewes unawares. No doubt the bastard had already taken up residence in his hunting box, and no doubt the kind of company he kept would prefer to be unobserved.

Nathan's lips twisted into a pleased smile. Whatever the journal contained could hang him, but what he knew could take Lewes and his contemporaries with him. If he were difficult about the diary, Nathan would threaten exposure but, just to be safe, he penned a note to an older and powerful acquaintance, Ambrose Manning, Duke of Staines, to outline his decision. Staines, a man more devious than Lewes and half of London altogether, would know how to act if the time came.

He collected a key from the very back of his desk drawer and tucked it securely in his pocket—the key to Lewes' hunting box. A key Lewes had likely forgotten Nathan still possessed. Before he departed his chamber, he entered his steward's office and brushed a hand over the back of Stackpool's chair. He missed the softly spoken 'good luck' Stackpool often uttered when Nathan was faced with a difficult battle.

Tonight, he would need all the luck he could get.

Nathan pulled his greatcoat higher up his chest, annoyed he'd forgotten to replace his white cravat for black. "Keep quiet and be prepared to leave swiftly when I return."

His coachman nodded, but his expression, faintly visible in the moonlight, appeared worried. "Aye, Your Grace. We'll be waiting."

He set off on foot for the distant house, the only habitable dwelling for miles. Thankful for his misspent youth, he navigated the distance easily enough and approached the house from the rear. Raucous laughter rang out and he stilled, glancing about the gardens and at the house windows to check he remained unobserved. The laughter rang out again and he eased closer once he'd determined the sound came from within.

Lights blazed in the east windows. Nathan pressed his back to the wall and listened. Inside, it appeared Lewes had invited his cronies to visit, but Nathan sensed he wouldn't like their games. As he shuffled along the wall, he caught a rough word now and again. From what he could tell the group was engaged in something scandalous, something obscene, and reluctantly Nathan peeked in the window.

A puff of putrid smoke filled his nostrils and he quickly covered his mouth before he coughed. Once he regained control over his senses, he risked another peek. As he suspected, Lewes had brought some of his cronies with him, men Nathan stored in his memory for later reference. By the look of them, they had some poor bastard on his knees.

The man took a fist to his ribs and the groan reached

Nathan's ears. The man, missing the lower half of his attire, slumped to the ground. Nathan winced as another man fell upon him. He turned away. Although he engaged in similar activities with men, he'd never once forced a man to bend over for him. He'd always enjoyed cooperative partners, no matter the urgency of his need. What occurred within these walls was beyond Nathan's sensibilities. It sickened him.

Unfortunately, with so many fellows within the house, he feared he'd never be able to make use of the front door key. Frustrated, he crept to another window, one darker than the rest. He couldn't open it.

The voices inside rose to a chant and then wild applause broke out.

"I say we keep him," said one. "Lewes has a chamber upstairs fitted with manacles. We can truss him up for more comfortable pleasure."

Nathan winced.

After a long debate, silence fell.

When Nathan crept back to the open window and saw the group leave through the opposite door. Reconciled that this may be his only choice, he listened carefully, then wedged his fingers under the window and lifted. The pane slid up silently. Nathan hauled himself inside, slid the pane closed and ducked behind the curtain. The room stank with sickly sweet smoke and he recognized the stench as opium.

Astounded that Lewes had developed a taste for the white smoke, he reopened the window and gasped for cleaner air. He wouldn't be able to remain long within the house or else he could become befuddled. He'd have to be quick.

The man on the ground moaned and Nathan risked a peek.

A younger man's bottom faced him, but the pale skin was marked with the brands of torture. Red, angry stripes crisscrossed white skin and Nathan cursed.

Despite the risks, he couldn't leave this man here. Not once he'd seen his plight.

Nathan heard no indication that the others would return. He took another two paces closer to the man on the ground and froze, unable to believe his eyes.

CHAPTER FOUR

A deep voice growled in Henry's ear and then all movement ceased. After a short pause the heavy weight pressing on his back shifted and he could breathe again. Voices rose behind him.

It was over, but for how long?

If he had the strength, he would get off the floor. Henry usually had more dignity than this. Not today. If he had heeded his initial instincts, he would have run from the Duke of Lewes the first chance he'd found. But he'd been arrogant and foolish. He had no one to blame but himself for his predicament.

He needed to leave.

He needed to be left alone long enough to formulate a plan, to acquire the ability to think without the ever-present stink of opium clouding his mind.

The deep voices rose in heated debate and then raucous laughter filled the air.

"I say we keep him," said one. "Lewes has a chamber upstairs fitted with manacles. We can truss him up for more comfortable pleasure."

Henry whimpered and the group laughed again. He cringed, waiting for hands to touch him. Nothing. The men discussed their comfort at length, but then the sounds moved away, their intent unclear over the scuffle of boots.

Silence. Blessed peace remained.

Henry breathed deep. The heavy scent of white smoke still permeated the room and he longed for cleaner air. He lifted his head again and looked about, but he couldn't see much. The numerous legs of drawing room furniture blocked his vision and then his gaze snagged on a pair of polished black boots.

They were empty, possibly discarded by another guest, yet their commonplace presence soothed. When they moved, Henry's panic returned threefold and he had to stifle a scream.

Black boots, black legs. All he could see was darkness coming for him. They approached silently; no sound would alert the previous occupants of the room that their territory was under threat, unless he managed to raise enough of a fuss, enough strength, to fight off this one remaining man.

But he didn't want His Grace's companions to come back. He didn't want the black boots to come closer either. They paused mere inches from his body and then Henry heard low-pitched cursing. This dark spirit, towering high above his limited view, cursed him in the worst possible way.

Henry couldn't hide. He had no strength to scuttle away and protect himself. The cursing stopped and then strong hands grabbed him. They pulled him upright with no apparent effort and held him against a warm body. Not a spirit; a man. If his nose wasn't filled with the stench of white smoke he might find comfort in the scent of this new presence. But he had no sense of smell, only touch and fallible sight. His lifted his eyes to where the face should be, but he glimpsed only a fantasy: an impossibility.

Henry's fantasy man forced his arms into the sleeves of a dark greatcoat and, hoping the gesture heralded a rescue, he fumbled to help. He wasn't sure he sped the process, but he did try until he was bound tight, clenched against the stranger's side.

Instead of the door, his fantasy dragged him toward an open window and, to his horror, pushed him out feet first. Unfortunately, Henry had no strength to stand and his legs buckled, folding him to the damp earth like an empty grain sack. He groaned, dragging in the damp night air, scrambling to straighten his body from the awkward position.

Another curse blistered his ears and then those strong hands pulled him up, supporting him against more warmth. In the moonlight, his fantasy remained. His employer, the Duke of Byworth, held him close against his chest, his lower body pressed tight against Henry's uncovered cock. The itchy wool created an ache within Henry, and he had strength enough to produce a half-hearted cockstand.

The fantasy man's hips jerked back, but with surprising dexterity, Henry captured the dark face to determine how great the illusion was. He could feel stubble, warmth, and when he brushed his fingers against lips, a damp exhalation caressed them.

Heedless of the desire not to break the delusion, Henry pressed his lips against the fantasy. He hoped the real man didn't mind. After the nightmare of Lewes' hospitality, he needed to be in control, to enjoy a moment of true desire. He tasted a hint of brandy on the man's breath before the fantasy turned away, slung an arm around Henry's back and dragged him away from danger.

As they crossed a patch of moonlight, someone called out from behind. It was not clear enough for Henry to determine the words, but his rescuer tightened his grip and forced him to move faster. Unwilling to return to the house he'd been trapped in, Henry tried to keep pace. He tripped, but was swept up and carried into the protective darkness of a stand of trees.

Hidden beneath the greatcoat, Henry started to shiver, suddenly afraid of where his fantasy man was taking him. A whimper snuck out before he could stop it.

The man holding him pulled him closer. "Damn it, keep quiet."

Henry curled into the warmth of the man, willing, daring to believe he was a rescuer. He looped his arms around the man's neck and pressed his face into the tight folds of a knotted white cravat. The man holding him breathed hard. Henry stayed silent, but his lips strayed upward and found a whiskered jaw to kiss.

Whoever he was didn't matter. He was delicious. Henry rasped his tongue along the rough jaw line and then flicked along the softer skin below.

The man twisted his head to dislodge Henry's lips and breath crossed his skin. Henry purred and attempted another kiss, but the stranger juggled him lower so his lips couldn't reach skin then dragged him off into the night at a greater pace. The jarring force of his speed reminded Henry that he hurt a great deal and he licked his lips, prepared to ask for respite.

Abruptly, their speed changed. He heard the faint jostle of horses and tack, the creak of a carriage, and the whispered hail of another man.

"There is a change of plan." A deep voice rumbled above Henry. "Take us to the cottage instead."

"'cor, blimey," another man exclaimed. "Is that who I think it is?"

Henry didn't hear the reply. He was too caught up in misery as hard leather seats embraced his aching body. He moaned, uncaring if his fantasy man would wish him silent still. The great coat fluttered around him then settled. Something else pressed over that. He rocked with the motion of the carriage, fighting to ignore the pain, and the only sound he heard was their steady passage along the road and rough breathing close by.

Henry was so used to heavy breathing by now that the uneven gasps didn't concern him. He wasn't hearing lust, only fatigue. Relief pierced his terror and he peered through his unruly hair.

This night-dark fantasy had saved him. His hair slipped away from his eyes and he could see again, although with the carriage lights unlit he was deprived of clarity. Flickering moonlight still tricked him into thinking his savior was his employer. The man knelt on the floor between the bench seats, watching Henry with concern the real duke would not.

Since he dreamed the most devastatingly attractive man he'd ever met hovered over him, Henry took matters into his own hands, determined to experience it all. Who knew when someone repulsive would replace this handsome image?

He licked his lips and the man leaned closer. Henry freed one arm, hooked his fingers around the man's neck and drew the stranger downward.

The man scowled, but Henry cradled that dark face, pulled those lips close enough to feel breath cross his and kissed the phantom duke as he'd longed to do since he first began working for him.

At first, his fantasy resisted. Henry didn't particularly care for that. Since this was his dream, he freed his other hand and pulled the man closer to set about breaching his defenses. His insistence seemed to attract the other man's complete attention. A tongue touched his and the phantom duke took over the embrace.

That was probably a good idea.

Although he didn't want the dream to end, Henry was weary. The rocking carriage was lulling him toward sleep when all he wanted to do was ride this sweet dream to its inevitable conclusion. The hot, open-mouthed kisses devoured him as if the other man were starving.

All Henry had to do was respond.

CHAPTER FIVE

Nathan drew back as his employee's eyes fluttered shut. Stackpool's face slacked, lips parted but damp from his kisses. His steward slept, fingers slowly uncurling from Nathan's hair. He grasped Stackpool's wrists and tucked his arms below the greatcoat where he could stay warm for the journey.

Then he scrubbed the back of his hand across his lips. Still reeling from that kiss, he contemplated the ill man opposite. The thought of hours of silent travel were a balm to his shaking senses. He was afire with lust, but such a reaction wasn't natural for him to enjoy. It was downright dangerous to his health.

Henry Stackpool: his steward, his essential assistant. A man he'd thought would never kiss him with such passion, a man who had been beaten and buggered while he'd hidden out of sight. Anger coiled within him. He would make Lewes pay dearly for this.

But then he remembered that in his haste to retrieve Stackpool, he'd failed to locate his wife's diary. Nathan punched the seat beside him. Damn it all, he'd have to go back, but not before he had seen to Stackpool's welfare.

Across from him, his servant slept peacefully now. But there would come a time when he would remember what had been done to him and Nathan hoped the humiliation would not break him. Determined that he wouldn't lose Stackpool, he would avoid the subject of buggery entirely, unless his servant brought it up.

But that kiss, that insistent need of Stackpool's to be kissed, confused Nathan. Surely a man with normal desires did not go around kissing men even if they were under the influence of white smoke.

Family, responsibility, duty—all managed to drown out the confusion pounding through his body and he closed his eyes, thinking of his children's smiling faces and allowed the dark night to smother his desire.

He woke when the carriage stopped.

Dawn was a smudge of grey on the far horizon and he blinked to orientate himself. They were at his summer cottage, his retreat south of his ducal seat. The relentless pounding of waves upon the shore reached him and he drew in a deep cleansing breath.

This place was his refuge—the home of his heart. Here Nathan could be himself without the responsibilities that came with the dukedom. He didn't get a chance to come here enough.

A glance at his companion showed Stackpool still slept, one hand curled beneath his cheek the other clutching the blanket tight. The sight of his steward lying so defenseless stabbed at him and he eased out of the carriage to speak to his coachman.

The driver peered around Nathan, trying to catch a glimpse of the sleeping man. "That is Mr. Stackpool. Is he going to die?"

Gossiping servants could be a problem. He didn't want word of Henry's misadventure to be a source of speculation amongst them. "I doubt there will be any lasting infirmity, but hear me well. I want no word of his illness to pass your lips. Given his duties with my children, I'll keep him away from them to spare them the distress of witnessing his bruises. Do you understand me?" Nathan dug in his waistcoat pocket and handed over coins. "I'll need you to get provisions for our stay."

The coachman nodded rapidly.

"Once you have the house opened, fires lit, and provisions fetched, I will require you to return to Grantley Park and obtain sufficient clothing for my stay."

"What about Mr. Stackpool?"

Nathan pursed his lips. "Obtain the bare necessities he needs from his chamber without being noticed, but if you have difficulties he can wear something of mine."

He blinked at Nathan's suggestion. "Yes, Your Grace. I'll be quick about it."

"Get some water heating. I'm sure Mr. Stackpool's cuts require attending."

The coachman took a last look toward the coach and then went on his way. When Nathan's servant was safely removed from the carriage's vicinity, he stepped back in to wake Stackpool.

His steward blinked groggily and ignored attempts to rouse him. But the frightened whimper he uttered in his sleep tugged at Nathan's little used heart. He pressed his finger against Stackpool's lips.

The other man quieted.

On impulse, Nathan brushed his steward's long hair from his eyes. Lashes fluttered, but he didn't wake. He considered that pale, serious face, familiar, yet distinctly not, and removed his hand. Sitting back, he contemplated his servant's appearance. Whatever must the coachman think of his bare feet and legs sticking out of the blanket? Not to mention the bare arse beneath. Stackpool's trousers had been nowhere in sight when Nathan had found him, and he'd had little time to look around.

For now, the opium he'd been fed would blot out the pain. Tomorrow, and the days following, Stackpool would be in agony.

Nathan pulled the blanket off Stackpool and slid his arms around the cloak-wrapped bundle. Stackpool stirred, rippling against Nathan's chest with a contented sigh. The sound made him think of kisses: languid, liquid heat shifting between their frantic tongues. Stackpool was one hell of a kisser. Even high on the opium they'd fed him, he'd devastated Nathan.

Trapping his burden close to his chest, Nathan

navigated the doorway and crossed the drive. He had them inside the sitting room in a moment. Stackpool moaned as Nathan settled him onto a dust cloth-covered settee. He scrounged for a blanket in a corner trunk and covered him over. The man burrowed into the cushions; asleep again in moments, but the sour stench of white smoke clung to him.

Warmth, this time liquid and comforting, slid over his skin in seductive waves. Henry was floating, it seemed, but there was movement against him.

Hands, gentle and thorough, glided over his skin, cupped his balls and cock briefly then slid down his legs. He wanted more touch to his cock. He wanted pleasure.

Although it was difficult, he opened his eyes and tried to focus on the room around him. A hearth fire burned hot and a copper tub held him suspended in deep water. This dream had turned practical. He could laugh he supposed, but that required effort he didn't want to expend. His feet were moved, tantalizing sensations raising gooseflesh and awakening a part of him that always begged like a hungry dog for scraps of attention.

He turned his head to see who teased him.

His fantasy man hadn't changed much. Regal, but disheveled. He remained trapped in a fantasy about his duke, his lord and master. But he wasn't Henry's. He'd never be naked around the morally upright Duke of Byworth.

Henry didn't know how long his fantasy would last and he grew desperate to extend the pleasure. He grabbed the hand holding the washcloth and brought it to his groin. Slippery hands fumbled, but he held them firm against his quickening flesh. And then mercifully, the fingers moved, curling around his aching length, granting blessed friction.

Overwhelming need rocked him.

Since Henry was dreaming, he had no qualms about letting his fantasy duke service him. The duke appeared good at it, too. He tightened his fingers and increased the pace, pulling pleasure up from Henry's toes. The impostor licked his lips. Henry caught His Grace's hair and pulled. The duke grunted and Henry received a brief kiss. Too little. He needed more. Henry parted his lips and sought more, pressing ardent kisses to a mouth slack with surprise. But then his fantasy lord dragged in a groaning breath and returned the gesture, hard, desperate kisses that made Henry's head spin.

Their tongues touched; each eager to dominate the exchange. He was too tired to tussle for long and he let the other man lead. The duke kissed his jaw, his neck, but returned to kiss his lips to obliterate all thought bar one.

Henry wanted to spend in that pretty mouth. He wanted his cock nestled deep when his pleasure peaked, so he twisted, threaded his fingers into the dark locks and tugged the fantasy man's head toward the water's surface.

The man resisted, his grip softening on his aching length.

"Suck me," Henry hissed. The dark head under his hand shuddered and then his cockhead was lifted above the water.

Warm breath stole over the tip. Shuddering, Henry widened his knees, tilting his hips in anticipation. Lips pressed to his cock and then the man tongued his slit. Blinding lust controlled Henry's arm and he pushed against the dark head again. The scorching heat of a hungry, wet mouth enveloped his cockhead and extended down over his aching length. As the man struggled to take in more, tongue lapping at his shaft to ease the way, Henry's cock thickened further.

The slow descent fired his pulse to dangerous levels and he clutched the dark locks to stay grounded. When lips enclosed most of him, Henry could do nothing except moan. His cock was buried deep, a tongue lapped at his length and then the man pulled back, to bob up and down in earnest. Delicious wet friction opened Henry's eyes as the other man wrung pleasure from every nerve.

Cheeks hollowed as the duke sucked hard, and Henry had never seen a prettier sight. His fantasy duke was good. He devoured him whole, kept his desires bubbling beneath the surface of his skin for a long time. Determined to enjoy the bounty within reach, he slid a hand over the other man's back and closed on a firm, fleshy arse. A deep needy moan vibrated through Henry's cock from his lover and his excitement spiked, exploding into blinding heat as he filled the Duke of Byworth's throat.

CHAPTER SIX

Wholly hell, he was mad. Nathan rocked onto his heels, and stared at the limp cock he'd just devoured. It lay not quite flaccid on a bed of pale curls, bobbing beneath the soapy bath water and tempting him again. He wiped his damp face, and glanced at Stackpool.

His steward had passed out, head turned to the side, mouth slightly open. He didn't snore, but his breath sounded terrifyingly loud in the empty cottage.

Anyone could have walked in and caught them. "Hell."

Stackpool flinched, sliding deeper into the copper tub until the water lapped under his chin. Not wanting him to drown, Nathan hooked his hands under Stackpool's arms and pulled. Bathwater tumbled from Stackpool's skin and drenched Nathan's legs. The cloudy gaze of his steward focused and he smiled suddenly, appearing blindingly happy to see Nathan.

Cock throbbing in earnest, Nathan fought the desire to kiss his servant again. He had to get him squared away and out of sight. Stackpool was heavy and slick. Yet as ungainly as he was, Nathan managed to maneuver him into a hard chair.

Stackpool hissed as his weight settled.

"Sorry." Grabbing up the length of towel, Nathan hurried to dry him, wiping gently over marks and scrapes that would ache like the devil soon. "Damn it, Stackpool. What the devil were you doing with the Duke of Lewes?"

He hoped for a response, but got nothing for his patience. Sighing, he threw the towel and hefted Stackpool over his shoulder like a sack of grain. It was helpful that his servant was light, but after traversing half the staircase, sweat poured off Nathan in waves. He was getting weak. Either that or he was getting old. To preserve his ego, he settled on the former. He was only three and thirty.

Feeling the other man slipping, Nathan clapped his hand over Stackpool's rear. His servant hissed in pain. Carefully, Nathan spread his fingers wide over the other man's bare backside and negotiated the remaining stairs without causing further aggravation. The morning sun streamed through the open window and he gratefully deposited Stackpool on the only decent bed in the house. His.

Nathan leaned over him, tucking him beneath the thick linen sheets of his hastily made bed to rest. Poor fool. He'd curse the day when he crossed paths with the Duke of Lewes. He lingered while Stackpool fell asleep. His steward lay caressed by sunshine, yet he'd been found in the darkest place Nathan knew, an establishment whose veneer of respectability was too thin by far.

When Stackpool whimpered suddenly, Nathan laid a hand upon his servant's bare shoulder. He stilled and Nathan rubbed small circles between the angry red marks that would turn purple and black eventually.

Not trusting himself to linger without molesting Stackpool, Nathan left the room and descended the staircase. The coachman had returned.

"Got everything you needed, Your Grace. Larder's full and if it's all right with you, I'll tend Mr. Stackpool before seeing to your supper."

"Stackpool is sleeping," Nathan said quickly, determined to prevent anyone seeing what had become of the other man. "I've tended his wounds."

Although the coachman raised an eyebrow at Nathan's words, he knew better than to question him.

Pleased that his title could be useful, Nathan dug in his pocket again. "After you've seen to supper and retrieve my possessions from Grantley, take yourself back to the village and spend the night at the inn. You may return in the morning, but I don't want to hear that you wrecked the tavern like last time."

The other man lowered his chin and muttered, "The man was rude."

Nathan sighed. His coachman was something of a hothead, yet he wanted him far from his sight until his steward was himself again. "Nevertheless, we might be here as long as a week. Do not wear out your welcome or you'll be sorry for it."

"A week." The coachman rubbed his hands together, anticipation evident in his smile. "Then I've got plenty of time to visit the widow on Rose Street. Always hinted I could stay for a bit if I wanted." The coachman tipped his hat and hurried out the door.

Nathan stood at the back door until he had disappeared and then he walked out to the cliff.

The cottage stood on a high bluff, offering views of the ocean and occasional passing ships. This place was his refuge. He came here to escape his wife and his responsibilities, but he wasn't alone this time. He had company. Delicious, masculine company.

That thought settled him to the ground and he hung his head, ashamed of what he'd done this morning. He'd taken a man's cock deep into his throat. He'd greedily sucked in the ridged flesh, tasted the salty musk and brought Stackpool pleasure. But he'd done it all without Stackpool being clearheaded enough to grant permission.

What made it worse was that Nathan had enjoyed it. And he wanted to do it again. Now. He wanted to taste all of his servant and never stop. It was wrong to think like those brutes at Lewes' house. He wasn't like them—he wasn't depraved, and Stackpool's head was turned by a girl in a pretty dress, not the cut of a man's waistcoat.

The sun stood high when Nathan returned to the house, but he was no closer to purging his soul of the unnatural desire to pleasure his servant again. He crept upstairs. Stackpool slept deeply, not even stirring when Nathan placed a hand upon his hot skin. Afraid of his own desires, he backed away and descended to the small sitting room. His book lay where he'd left it on his last stay so he tucked it under his arm and headed outside to read.

Several times he checked on Stackpool. His servant moved a bit but stayed deeply asleep, hair tossed across his cheek until Nathan swept it back with his thumb. As the sun set he entered the kitchen. A stew bubbled on the hearth, and Nathan lifted the lid, assailed by the most delicious smell. But he was starved for more than food. He wanted Stackpool awake.

He had an alarming need to hear his steward speak of his ordeal and confirm he was well. Nathan awkwardly scooped out two generous bowls of stew, tucked a loaf of bread under his arm, and hurried upstairs.

Henry could smell stew. The scent wafted under the sheet he'd pulled up over his face and teased him. His stomach rumbled, but he couldn't determine if it was in anticipation or some other malady.

Silver clinked against porcelain and he eased the sheet lower. Still deep in fantasy, the Duke of Byworth watched from the dark edge of the room. There was no hint of welcome, only silent contemplation. Henry couldn't keep his eyes on a delusion so he glanced around the dim chamber. A plain, square room, window sealed tight against the outside world. Henry didn't recognize the dwelling and he turned back to the apparition. His Grace stood beside the bed now, hands empty of spoon or bowl. Perhaps Henry merely dreamed.

"Mr. Stackpool."

Henry gulped. Familiar voice—familiar greeting. "Your Grace." So, this wasn't a dream. It was a nightmare.

"How are you feeling?"

Henry had to think about it for quite a while. His brain didn't want to catalogue anything but fatigue. He thought about his toes, legs, his arse hurt, his stomach cramped, his ribs ached. "I am well."

The duke snorted and laid a hand across Henry's forehead. Now that the duke brought it to his attention, Henry was fever hot and drenched in sweat. He couldn't understand why.

"Ah, you've developed a trickster's tongue have you?" The aristocratic quirk of one eyebrow confirmed he was speaking to the duke and he had the uncomfortable feeling that he blushed. He hoped the fever would disguise his reaction to his employer's gentle caress. "Can you sit up?"

It was an interesting question. Henry didn't want to, but his habit of obeying the duke made the request impossible to ignore. As he struggled upright, Byworth hooked his hands under Henry's arms and sped his movement. When he let go, the weight of his body pressed his backside into the bedding. A hiss of pain escaped his lips.

He rolled sideways and didn't dare look at his employer. The pain brought back memories of his time with the Duke of Lewes. Humiliation washed over him. His Grace, the Duke of Byworth, would have a fair idea of why he was in pain and Henry waited to hear his condemnation.

"As I expected," his master muttered darkly.

He supposed he was revolted with him, yet why was he here? Surely, he could have dumped him elsewhere: far away from him.

The duke circled the bed and sat on the side Henry faced. He didn't say anything else, only held out a mug of ale. Henry swallowed a few large mouthfuls, but His

Grace took it out of reach fairly soon. Next came a hunk of bread and Henry gobbled it up, eager for more. The duke left the bed, but returned with a bowl of stew.

Henry had to meet the duke's gaze. His Grace wouldn't give him the spoon. Dark eyes should have poured scorn on his head, yet they held an odd gleam. His whole face reflected an emotional state with which Henry was unfamiliar.

He glanced about him nervously. "Where are we?"

"We are at the cottage."

CHAPTER SEVEN

Their location surprised Henry. The duchess claimed the cottage a hovel, yet the room was clean and smelled only of the sea. He pulled a deep breath into his lungs as he listened for the pounding waves beyond the walls. There. He hadn't noticed it before, but the house seemed to vibrate with the soothing sound. He let his breath escape. With the drapes drawn against the night, he couldn't see beyond the window. Part of him longed to get out of bed and hurry outside to see the ocean he'd only heard about. The sensible part suggested that the excursion could wait.

The duke cleared his throat. "We'll talk later. Eat now."

Henry obediently ate what the other man offered, barely more than the duke's youngest child would manage, yet his stomach felt as if it would burst. When he couldn't eat another mouthful, His Grace crossed the room, picked up a book and ignored him.

Uncertain of what his behavior signified, Henry sank into the bedding once more and studied him. The Duke of Byworth was a conservative man. If he had one glimmer of understanding of what Henry truly was then he'd be hauled before the magistrate and then the hangman's stage.

The duke stirred in his chair like a restless cat. Usually, his placid countenance soothed, but tonight Henry churned in the grip of lust. Despite the pain of his abused flesh, his cock hardened, lengthening under the sheet beyond his power to control. He rolled over, away from the arousing sight of His Grace stretching. The fantasy he'd dreamed about many a night was a dangerous one to cultivate. He pulled the blankets tight around him, suddenly chilled through.

The duke's chair creaked again and the room grew dark. Fabric rustled and then the bed dipped behind him as His Grace lay down. Henry couldn't breathe and he certainly wasn't going to turn over and ask his master what he was about. He had the most painful erection of his life and all he wanted to do was rub his cock against his employer's body.

The duke sighed. "Stackpool?"

"Yes, Your Grace."

"Are you feeling any better?"

Was he feeling better? He had no idea. He couldn't feel anything beyond lust. "I don't know."

A warm hand brushed his shoulder and then swept over his face. "You're chilled. You should have said something."

The duke fussed with the blankets, but then settled his hand between Henry's shoulder blades. That hot spot of warmth kept him aroused until fever swept over him again and he struggled out of the sheets. It was a good thing the hot flushes cooled his ardor because the duke hovered over him all through the long night. Cooling him by flicking off the sheets, heating him with a simple touch; he'd never felt so cosseted in his life.

When morning broke, he was tired, but the fever and chills had passed. As he blinked sleep from his eyes, a large, warm hand slid off his belly as the duke turned onto his back. Henry gulped. Could his master tell he'd woken aroused? He prayed desperately he had not.

Discovery of his lust would only speed Henry's journey to the hangman.

The duke rolled out of bed and fumbled around in the half-light. Thin lines of sunlight filtered through the gaps in the drapes and Henry caught brief glimpses of his master's naked body. In particular, he noted Byworth's cock standing at attention with morning arousal. God, he was beautiful. Henry's mouth watered.

He tried to keep quiet. The sight of that thick length made his arse clench in anticipation, yet he was in no state to consider lovers of any kind. Even lying down, he throbbed and knew that sitting for any length of time would prove problematic. He feigned sleep as Byworth pulled open the drapes and sunshine fell into the room.

Blinking rapidly to pretend the glare had woken him, Henry tried to keep his focus on the other man's face. His Grace quirked his lips a little hesitantly and Henry dropped his gaze to the man's chest. Thick with muscle, not a spare pound of flesh in sight, he let his gaze graze and dream that he might touch that sun kissed skin. That one day he might rest his head upon his flat abdomen and nuzzle Byworth's thickened cock into his mouth.

The duke moved closer and Henry almost reached for his employer, yet the other man merely grabbed his pillow and made a show of removing the dent his head had made. Ignoring an upstanding cock, displayed in his line of sight, was never an easy task. The fully aroused length didn't do anything but make Henry want. He licked his lips as His Grace turned away and began covering himself with clothes.

It was hard not to be disappointed. The duke was a fine specimen, fit and densely muscled. And his heavy cock would be so sweet across his tongue. He wanted him in his hand. He wanted to kiss the Duke of Byworth so badly his head spun.

The duke rushed from the room.

Startled by his abrupt departure, Henry looked around. As he glanced toward his feet, he realized his erection would have been noticeable.

His poor master. Henry bet the other man was disgusted. He rolled over onto his belly and breathed in the scent of His Grace's skin imprinted on the sheets. His cock throbbed and he ground his hips into the bedding, letting his mind conjure images of the duke beneath him. He rocked his hips, again and again, until he heard the door click shut behind him.

Horrified, caught with his arse in the air and an erection burrowing into the bedding, Henry stayed still.

Soft footsteps came closer. A hand touched his calf. "The cuts have bled again."

The duke's softly uttered observation stopped his heart. Lewes, that sick perverted monster, had taken a whip to him for refusing to provide the information he wanted. The leather had quickly cut through Henry's trousers and the biting sting had made him scream. But to know that his master inspected his injuries proved a humiliation he'd never expected.

The sound of water being poured into a basin echoed in the silence. He buried his head in his pillow as the duke patted over the welts. Yet the humiliation did nothing to control his arousal.

"Widen your legs," the duke requested.

God, he was going to explode. The duke softly patted the damp cloth around his inner thighs, then lower to brush his stones. Henry couldn't control his reaction and he came from just that slight teasing. Pleasure burst from every nerve in his body and as he returned to earth, he realized the duke still cleaned him, paying particular attention to his stones as they descended again.

How the duke could ignore that he had just spent? The sheet fluttered over his body and the Duke of Byworth left him alone.

❧

Nathan peeked through the gap between door and hinges, waiting for his steward to climb into bed and cover himself. After the events of half an hour ago he didn't know what he'd face. He shouldn't have caressed his steward the way he had, even if his actions provoked an interesting response.

That Stackpool had soiled the sheets excited him. He glanced down at his impatient cock and rubbed his hand hard across it. The desire to test the waters and see if Stackpool truly desired the touch of another man held sway until he got a good look at his steward's poor battered body.

There were bruises on Stackpool's ribs and hips. Ugly purple shades that made Nathan's blood boil in anger, dousing his lust in seconds. Over some were whip marks. He wanted to beat the life out of Lewes for losing control, yet he couldn't leave Stackpool just yet. Not until he was certain the other man was well.

When his servant lingered at the window, Nathan grew impatient. He squared his shoulders and walked in. "Are you hungry?"

The expression on Stackpool's face was priceless. His skin flushed, gaze quickly darting downward, then snapping back to Nathan's face. Intrigued, he placed the tray on the bed and took a step in his servant's direction.

Stackpool's bare cock filled, thickened until his impressive length stood tall. Nathan's own flesh responded in kind. Pleased that his servant was attracted to men, or at least to him, he'd see whether Stackpool's employment could be altered to include the occasional pleasure once he had recovered his health.

Nathan could wait as long as needed.

He crossed to where Stackpool had stilled like a hunted fox. Nathan smiled and the other man seemed to come alive again. He hurried across the room, slid beneath the covers, attempting to hide his body's response.

Nathan followed, draping himself across the foot of the bed, watching as Stackpool made a show of eating. "What the devil were you doing with Lewes?"

"I, ah, was invited to dine with him," Stackpool stammered.

"It is not like Lewes to entertain the common man without some form of compensation changing hands. Were you there by your own wish?"

Stackpool shifted. "Of course I was."

Nathan gestured to the bruises encompassing the other man's arms. "And these marks of restraint? Were they willingly accepted?"

At that, Stackpool finally appeared uncomfortable. Would he lie? "No. But Lewes never made them."

Nathan shuffled down the bed, arranging his body more comfortably. "Of course not. His habits are simpler, direct. Like the whip marks on your skin. No doubt that bruise forming on your jaw is courtesy of him. Did you try to leave?"

The other man dropped his head. "No. He wanted information."

Nathan sat up, leaning forward toward his servant. "About whom?"

Up close, Stackpool's green eyes, flecked through with gold, mesmerized him.

"About an old friend of mine."

Nathan rubbed his jaw, considering. "In all the time you've worked for me I've never heard you mention friends or family for that matter. Where do you hail from?"

"London."

He'd known that. That was where they had first met. "Where is your family?"

Stackpool sighed. "Dead. I've taken care of myself since I was seven."

Now that was news to Nathan. If he remembered correctly, there had been a glowing reference from several respectable Londoners, all attesting to Stackpool's character and reliability. There was no mention of him being an orphan. "And this friend of yours Lewes is so interested in. Who exactly is he to you both?"

"A friend, and a whore."

"A woman?" Nathan was surprised. Lewes had little use for women. He couldn't imagine him searching for one unless he'd been swindled.

Stackpool's face reddened. "Rather than have you guessing all day until you get your damn answers, I'll get this over with. My friend is a whore from London's Hunt Club, a place where I worked until I entered your service."

Nathan stilled as his mind connected Hunt Club with a distant memory. "Hell's teeth, I'm a founding member of that club. Were you employed there?"

CHAPTER EIGHT

Henry flinched. Byworth knew of the Hunt Club's male companions. Heart pounding, he wriggled off the bed and searched for his trousers. When he didn't find them, he turned around. "Where are my clothes?"

The duke sat up and swung his legs over the side of the mattress. "Below stairs. Half of them anyway. They stink of white smoke."

Uncomfortable with standing naked before his employer, Henry grabbed a pillow and set it before his groin. "If you will excuse me, Your Grace, I'll be on my way."

As Henry passed the duke, breath churning with anxiety, His Grace caught his arm. "Get back into bed. I cannot have you prowling the house in that state. The coachman might return at any moment."

He hesitated. The duke stroked his thumb over Henry's arm. He glanced sideways and caught his master gazing at his bare bottom. Startled, he turned so the pillow stood between him and Byworth. "I think, perhaps, I should be on my way before you send for my executioner."

"No executioner." The duke tugged Henry toward him. "You're much too handsome for the long drop."

Henry's mouth fell open.

The duke tugged his arm again, sending Henry staggering toward the bed head. "Get your arse back in bed, Stackpool, before I do something incredibly stupid."

Henry dove under the sheets, hiding his erection as best he could. Yet his heart thudded with the knowledge that Byworth knew his inclinations and didn't care enough about them to raise a fuss.

A surge of relief passed through his heart. He may not have to leave Grantley Park. He may not need to live in fear any longer that his employer would learn of his inclinations and dismiss him. He'd still have to take great pains to remain respectful and keep his desires well under control. However, even with those conditions, a great weight lifted from his shoulders. He smiled suddenly, then schooled his features to polite subservience again.

"Tell me how you came to be at Lewes' estate?"

The duke's calm question whipped Henry from his ruminations. He licked his lips, debating whether he should keep secrets. Given Byworth knew of his past, and hadn't thrown him out, he elected to tell the truth. "We met at the village by accident, and he invited me to join him at his hunting box."

"Invited? That doesn't sound like the Duke of Lewes I'm acquainted with."

Henry grimaced. "Perhaps invited was too mild a word, but to refuse him would have drawn attention. I had intended to slip away unnoticed later."

The duke scowled. "After he, and his cronies, had their way with you?"

Even after all this time, a hot flush crept over Henry's cheeks. "Lewes never touched me that way. I wasn't agreeable to his demands."

The duke stared. Usually his appraisal caused only a momentary rush of desire that he could control, yet today there was an odd edge to the glance. Eventually, Byworth nodded and glanced away. "You should rest. I'll have your clothes returned after Brown launders them."

Henry sat up as he remembered his only good luck of the past night. "Don't launder them. Bring them to me."

"No." The duke stood. "I'll not bring that stench up here."

"Please, Your Grace, you can throw them out the window when I'm done but I must see them now. It's very important."

Although the duke frowned, he left the chamber while Henry fidgeted to get comfortable. He hoped that his suffering had been worthwhile. He hoped he hadn't lost the duchess' diary.

The duke hurried in, arm held before him, and tossed a messy pile of cloth to Henry. He quickly found his waistcoat, ran his hands over the lining, and touched paper. "Thank heavens." Henry pulled the torn pages from a slit he'd cut and made a stack on the bed. "The duchess' diary, Your Grace, sans cover. I'm afraid I had to excise the sheets."

The duke plucked the pages from the mattress and shuffled through them. "Did you read any of this?"

"Other than determining the authenticity of the handwriting, I did not. That is every page written by the duchess' hand. I left the cover and blank pages behind to delay Lewes' discovery of the theft."

The duke's deep sigh rattled through the room. "Stackpool, what would I do without you? You are the most loyal and selfless man I know."

Before he could stammer out a reply the duke crossed the room, clutched Henry's skull, and kissed him full on the mouth. For a moment, Henry was too stunned to react. But the duke teased his tongue along the seam of his lips, he opened his mouth and kissed him back. Pleasure fizzled along every nerve as the duke bore him to the mattress and continued his tender assault.

Henry shuddered as the duke drew away, wariness swiftly replacing his desire.

The duke, however, only stared at the pages in his hand. "Thank you for these."

Byworth turned away, dragged a chair toward the window and bent his head to read, leaving Henry more confused than ever.

However, one thing stood out clearly in his mind. The duke had enjoyed that kiss: his trousers appeared quite snug in the front.

"You should eat." The duke waved the papers in the air. "This could take a while."

He held the beautiful man's gaze as long as he could, but he knew a blush was flooding his cheeks. "Yes, Your Grace."

But the sudden dismissal cut. To hide his discomfort, Henry fixed his attention to the heaped tray. When he had finished every bite, the duke was still reading so, with no other demands on his time, he lay back against the pillows and closed his eyes against his body's aches and pains.

The summer light was fading from the sky as the bed dipped. With a start he realized he'd slept the afternoon away and he quickly glanced at the duke to see if he was in need.

The duke sighed and raked a hand through his hair, disturbing the precise waves. "We need to return to Grantley tomorrow. Will you be well enough to make the journey?"

Henry quickly took stock of his aches and pains. He nodded. "I will be ready when you desire to go."

The duke snorted. "I'd rather remain here, but—" he held up the remnants of the diary—"my duchess must be dealt with."

He looked up at his master sharply. "What has she done now?" Immediately, he regretted his demand for more information. It wasn't his place to question his employer, but he did care for his reputation. Given the duke's expression, the diary had contained something distasteful. When the duke never answered, Henry lowered his head. He shouldn't have asked. One soul-stirring kiss did not make them equals.

The duke brushed a hand over Henry's sheet-covered foot. "Are you hungry?"

Henry hastily slid his limb away. "No thank you, Your Grace."

Byworth shifted restlessly on the bed, rubbing a hand repeatedly across his upper thigh. Henry struggled to keep from staring. The master had impressively thick legs. He'd enjoyed the view for some time. "I'll return directly."

As helpful as any footman, the duke scooped up the tray and ruined clothing and disappeared out the door. When his steps had faded past hearing, Henry thumped his head against the pillow.

Fool. Despite that kiss, he should not lust after his employer. Byworth was a married man and, like most titled men, given to chasing light skirts when in Town. Resigned to giving up an impossible wish, he curled onto his side and attempted to fall asleep.

But sleep proved impossible. He was wide awake when Byworth returned to the chamber. Fabric rustled and then the room darkened, yet moonlight fell upon his face.

As the duke slipped into the bed behind Henry's back, desire clawed through him.

Byworth moved closer and settled a hand on his shoulder. When he applied greater pressure, Henry rolled onto his back. "Did I thank you properly for your devotion?"

Despite the dark, Henry ducked his chin as his face grew warm. He'd received a kiss for his trouble, but he selfishly wanted more.

His Grace's breath tickled Henry's cheek. "Thank you, Stackpool. You have saved me a great deal of embarrassment. But if you go near the Duke of Lewes again, I will paddle your narrow arse personally."

He rolled toward the duke. His head landed on Byworth's bent arm, and he was pulled into a tight embrace. He winced at the pressure over tender bruises, but the distraction of the duke brushing the hair from his eyes stifled his voice. The duke pressed his lips to Henry's cheek, then proceeded to kiss a path to his lips.

Sweet heavens, when the duke claimed his mouth in another soul-numbing kiss, Henry couldn't resist. He grasped Byworth's head roughly and slanted his mouth to deepen the embrace. When His Grace groaned, memories arose—a face touched by moonlight, dark hair threaded through his fingers and his wet hand pushing the duke down onto his cock.

Henry broke the kiss.

He hadn't dreamt the kiss before, he'd lived it. Lips brushed again and obliterated every thought in his head. Henry let Byworth have his way. Heat scalded him where they touched. The duke's hands were gentle, brushing over bruises, yet sweeping his body with hunger.

Henry's arse clamped tight in anticipation, but in doing so he was reminded that he wasn't capable of certain pleasures he normally wished for. Disappointment broke into his enjoyment. He pulled back from his employer with regret. Byworth followed, pushing him deep into the bedding and pressed his lips to his neck, hovering over his pulse.

He freed his arm from between them and draped it over the broad shoulders. Hard muscles shifted and moved as the duke repositioned to lick his nipples. Given the degree of attention he was receiving, Henry couldn't help but moan.

The duke chuckled. "Like that, do you?" Byworth fastened his lips over a peaked bud and sucked, his face burrowing into Henry's chest and setting his already over-wound nerves on fire.

"Yes," Henry gasped. He threaded his fingers through the duke's wavy hair. No dream this time. His employer pleasured him by moonlight.

Byworth's sudden caress against Henry's cock dragged a whimper from his throat. "I take it you like that too, Your Grace?"

Another gasp escaped as His Grace rapidly stroked him.

The duke leaned close. "Considering I'm about to stick your cock in my mouth again, Henry, you'd better call me Nathan."

CHAPTER NINE

Nathan couldn't hold back from Henry any longer. Especially not when he writhed on the bed in such obvious abandon. He stroked the hot cock in his hand, watching for the glint of wet seed at the tip. Henry's desire fuelled his own to an alarming degree and he couldn't resist swiping his tongue across the head, enjoying the gasp from the other man. His skin was like silk against his tongue, and Nathan suckled, attempting to gather as much of Henry's desire as he could.

Strong fingers curled into Nathan's hair as he kissed Henry's silky soft cockhead then continued lower. Poking out his tongue, Nathan nudged the stones around in the hairy sac, slurping back saliva as desire rode him hard. He was starving for Henry and he was more than happy when his servant widened his thighs.

Unable to resist, Nathan dropped his head between them and drew one of his stones into his mouth. The scandalous softness between his lips pulled a grunt from deep inside. He gently suckled the elusive nut, but it pulled up tight to his body, so he flicked his tongue over the tensed skin, licking the ridges until Henry groaned.

Determined to taste Henry again he rose to his knees over his cock. He slipped the tip just past his lips, letting the silky smooth head rest on his tongue. Henry groaned again, his fist pulled hard on Nathan's hair and he moaned as arousal thickened his cock.

Prying his servant's arousal upright, he fisted him with one hand, tongued his slit, before sliding his mouth down as low as it could go. Nathan gave Henry the same treatment he liked for himself and his servant responded with deep grunts and groans.

He settled into a steady rhythm, sucking and pulling until Henry's hips bucked, pushing his cock deeper into his mouth.

Henry tugged on Nathan's hair. "I'll spend soon."

He lifted up to tell him to wait, but Henry's hot release splashed across his face and lips. He lapped it quickly, eager not to miss a single drop of his seed.

His servant pulled their faces close. "You shouldn't do that."

"You taste good." Nathan kissed him, letting his cock rest against the other man's thigh.

Henry burrowed between them to grasp him.

Instinctively, Henry knew exactly how hard to squeeze. He roughly pumped Nathan's aching flesh and he groaned at the feel of Henry's experienced hand on his erection. Oh God, he was good.

Nathan let him stroke him toward a release he'd been dreaming of since he'd rescued him, since they'd first kissed, since they'd first met. He tried to hold back, but Henry snuck his other hand lower and palmed his balls, holding them between strong fingers. Nathan jerked and spilled over Henry's taunt, firm belly.

They both watched his release slide along Henry's pale skin in the moonlight. His lover captured the stream before it touched the sheet and brought his hand to his mouth to taste. Desire tightened Nathan's balls. "You don't have to do that."

"I wanted to taste you." Henry licked his fingers clean as he lay subdued against the pillows. "Lay on your belly for me."

Nathan hesitated, unsure what Henry had in mind. He shifted off his lover and rested his upper body on his arms. "Like this?"

Henry licked his lips. "Yes."

Confusion made him squirm, rubbing his sated cock against the bedding. Henry shifted further down the bed until he lay flat on his back. He trailed his hand across his own belly, coating his fingers with Nathan's seed.

Nathan held his breath as damp flesh brushed over his arse and then probed between his cheeks. Gasping at the ferocity of desire that climbed his spine once more, he thrust his hips against the bedding.

Henry smacked Nathan's bottom, hard. "None of that now, Nate."

Hearing his servant, his lover, whisper his name stilled the retort he wanted to utter. He hadn't been spanked since he was in short pants, yet the sensation was altogether different. Arousing, instead of humiliating.

Henry's probing intensified, pushing deeper between his cheeks to touch his entrance. Nathan stiffened and then groaned as his lover pressed harder, invading his depths. "Hmm... this won't do, up on your hands and knees, Your Grace."

Nathan mustn't have moved fast enough because Henry struck him hard on his backside, as if he had the right to. He groaned and assumed the position. "Is this what you want?" He didn't look at Henry. He thought he was blushing and grown men didn't blush, but dear God he found he liked the sweet pain of a little punishment.

"No." Another stinging slap. "Crawl until you are over the top of me."

Nathan set his hands level with Henry's ribs and bracketed him with his legs. His body hovered, thickening cock and heavy balls dangling directly over Henry's thighs.

"Move further up."

There was no slap this time, but he didn't need the punishment to become more aroused. He inched forward as Henry's damp fingers slid up from below, penetrated deeper into his arse. Nathan groaned as the invading fingers wiggled.

Henry fingered his arse at a slow pace, pausing to stretch his entrance, turning Nathan into a man only capable of grunting incoherently. He raised his gaze to see his lover. Henry's mouth twisted as he thrust his fingers, he paused and then greater pressure invaded his hole. Another finger, a thicker claiming. Henry lifted his chin and joined their mouths together.

Around Henry's lips, Nathan moaned, writhing on the invading fingers, but not wanting respite. Another pause as Henry shoved his tongue in his mouth and added more fingers to his already stretched entrance.

Henry held Nathan's pleasure in his two hands—fingers up his arse, the rest closing on his balls, tugging and driving him toward a familiar ecstasy. Without warning, the sensations stopped. "Sit down."

Nathan raised heavy eyes to Henry, but the man appeared completely serious. He lowered his arse, only to stop as he butted against his lover's upstanding cock. Was this the time to mention the absence of this aspect of lovemaking in recent years? "Henry?"

A stinging slap answered his question and he willed his body to keep going. There was resistance, and it stung, but Henry took his time and kept Nathan aroused as he worked to impale himself on the hard length.

His arse burned. Nathan took lovers—they didn't often take him. He held still, expecting another slap as punishment for stopping.

Henry's fingers skimmed across his belly. "That's it, Nate, just sit there and get used to me being inside you." His skin shone with sweat, his breath churned rough and fast. "Christ, your arse is sweet. You would tempt a vicar to debauch you if you gave one the chance."

Nathan shifted at the surprising compliment and Henry slid in further. He winced as his lover invaded, but Henry was patient, letting him adjust to the feel of him. With one hand he stroked Nathan's softened cock, with the other he pinched and squeezed Nathan's nipples until both were hard. He shuddered, opening a little further.

"Move now. I want to fuck you," Henry growled in a

deep commanding voice Nathan had never heard before from him.

The novelty of being ordered about excited him. Nathan squirmed a little. Henry slapped a stinging blow across his thigh and he moved. Sharp stinging pain made him wince as he gently worked himself on the stiff length. Eventually his body remembered that he enjoyed such pleasures but it had been a long time. Henry gripped his hips and then they moved as one; fucking Nathan from below with short even thrusts. He wrapped a hand around his own length, stroking in time to Henry's thrusts.

He leaned forward, resting one hand on Henry's bare chest and closed his eyes.

Henry's grip tightened, his short thrusts grew quicker. "Squeeze your arse."

Nathan gladly did as he was told. The burning thrill of invasion and his furious stroke on his cock pushed him over the edge. He tightened around the hard length and Henry shouted as he peaked. Warmth invaded Nathan's arse, while his seed streaked across Henry's skin again.

Nathan collapsed, uncaring of Henry's sweat damp skin and his release. When the other man's cock popped free, he wanted him back. He wanted that intense pleasure all over again.

Henry's soft groan filled his ears.

Nathan heaved himself upright to meet his steward's serious expression. "Sorry." He rolled over until he landed on his back, breath churning but uncertain what else he should say. He had rarely lain with a man in a bed before, usually he'd taken his pleasure in quick silent rendezvous, yet when Nathan had lain with another man he had known the other outside of it too. But Henry was his employee and they usually spoke only of business matters and infrequently of his children. What did one say after being intimate with an employee?

"I'm fine." Henry shifted. "Are you all right, Your

Grace?"

He turned his head. Henry's frown pierced his discomfort. "Perfectly well, thank you." As an afterthought he added, "And you?"

Henry's face split into a rare grin. "Never better, Your Grace."

Nathan laughed then ruffled his lover's hair. "Nate."

"Nate, then."

He shifted and drew Stackpool against him. "You do a good job of hiding your inclinations. I never suspected before yesterday."

The man in his arms stiffened. "I'd rather not hang."

"I quite agree." Nathan drew in a shuddering breath at the thought. Now that he had Henry close, he took advantage of his proximity to learn his contours. He shaped his hands carefully over his lover's back and bottom, careful to keep the pressure light and avoid aggravating the injuries. "I'd not like to lose you."

Henry pressed his lips to Nathan's chest. "I've been your man since the first day, Nate. I've no intention of leaving your service unless you dismiss me."

A bubble of excitement curled within Nathan at Henry's words. He had often wondered when, not if, he would leave. The knowledge his steward would remain a permanent fixture at Grantley curled his lips into a smile. "Just as well. The children would have become cross."

The man in his arms chuckled and squirmed closer. "They are wonderful children. You must be so proud to have them."

Nathan pressed another kiss to Henry's forehead. "I am. But you must come to me if they run you ragged. I'd not like their constant requests to affect your duties."

Henry stiffened, drawing away from Nathan. "Have you been dissatisfied with my performance so far, Your Grace?"

"Hardly." He captured Henry's hand and laid it upon his limp cock. A coil of pleasure stroked his spine as the other man's fingers curled tight around him. Nathan gasped. "Even more satisfied now."

CHAPTER TEN

Sunlight warmed Henry's back and he turned to savor the heat beating across his face. He didn't want to go home; he wanted to stay at the cottage forever. Deep contentment stole over him as he listened to the gulls calling from the bay. His lover needed to go home, but he wanted to stay here where they had privacy.

The real world lay in wait, ready to strangle the idyllic pleasures of the cottage. Beyond this secluded property a world of judgment hovered, ready to pounce and condemn them for their desires. Something Henry had feared all his life.

Nate's strong arm wrapped around his waist and pulled him tight against burning hot skin. Henry could never get enough of his lover's touch, but Nate was a duke, and as such, had responsibilities awaiting him at home.

Delicious pleasure swept over the back of his neck as Nate pressed his lips there. This would be the only time he could wake up beside his lover. At Grantley Park, his chamber was a narrow slice of room at one end of the attic, directly over the children's nursery. Nate couldn't risk being found there with him at any hour of the day. And Henry doubted he could steal into the duke's bedchamber without his ever-present valet finding out.

Nate's fingers wandered over his belly, caressing and causing Henry's cock to stir.

"Good morning."

"Good morning to you too. Did you sleep well?"

Nate stared down at him, a foolish grin marking his face. "Like the dead. I haven't slept so well in years."

Henry turned his body so their lips aligned and kissed his lover. Turning over also revealed Nate's arousal. Another thing they had in common. His own cock had ached since he'd first awakened. He settled Nate between his parted legs and kissed them both awake.

When Nate's lips slid from his and wandered to his neck, Henry had enough sense left to remember what plans they had. "We had better get a wriggle on. The coach might come early."

Nate found the perfect spot on Henry's neck to kiss and, as much as they should stop, Henry offered his throat so his lover could devote his attention to it. His skin tingled and his cock throbbed. Nate aroused him so easily. How would he survive at Grantley Park without being able to touch Nate again?

Nate drew back, grinning down at him with mischief in his eyes. "I told our coachman noon. That gives us," he squinted out the window, "at least three hours to play."

A smile tugged Henry's lips. Nate was voracious.

Henry threw him over onto his back and held him still when the duke protested. "Now then Your Grace, I believe you haven't learnt your proper place. On your back, both feet in the air, that is how I want you."

Nate's breath hitched. "I thought you had to obey me, Henry? I am the master of Grantley Park."

His smile faded. "You cannot rule everything in life. I accept your authority over my services during the day and you must accept mine at night."

"It is day now." Nate tried to throw him over, a half-hearted attempt but Henry held firm.

"Perhaps I should rephrase that. At night... or in bed."

Nate pulled Henry's head down. "What did I do before you came to manage me?"

"I imagine you were a trifle overbearing."

The duke growled at his audacity but brushed his cock against Henry's. His lover's expression changed. The slide of firm flesh distracted Nathan from his need to control. Rising above him, Henry stroked Nate's chest, swirling his fingers over his flat nipples. The buds tightened, peaked. He pinched them between his fingers and then tugged. Nate gasped. He liked his pleasure with a sting of pain, but not too much and that suited Henry perfectly.

Letting his nipples go, he dropped low and suckled him. Nate threaded his fingers through his hair, gasping as he held Henry's head in place. He caught Nate's flesh between his teeth and bit down lightly. Nate arched and then his hands delved between them.

Nate grasped Henry's cock and he set up a lazy stroke that sent pleasure soaring through every nerve. Henry moved backward, taking his cock out of Nate's reach and pressed his lips to Nate's damp cockhead. His lover grunted, sounding disappointed but excited just the same.

Taking his time, Henry nibbled down Nate's length, following the ridges and thick veins with the tip of his tongue. Nate drew his knees up and let them fall to the side, so Henry slipped his tongue down between his balls. Nate's groans grew louder as Henry took the slickened pouch between his lips and massaged with the flat of his tongue.

His lover groaned in earnest, his thighs trembling. Unwilling to have him spill too soon, Henry released him and kissed up Nate's hard length, letting his gaze catch Nate's. Face flushed, breathing ragged, the duke's eyes widened.

With slow, deliberate precision Henry inched his lips closer to Nate's cockhead. He dragged his mouth to the tip, then swirled his tongue in lazy passes over the tip. Nate stiffened as his teasing tongue pleasured him, then Henry opened his mouth wide and took him deep.

Nate's hips bucked immediately, fucking his mouth and working his cock deeper down his throat. When Henry had him swallowed down to the root, he held still, panting around the thick length. He loved swallowing all of Nate. He let the ridges and bulging veins slip over his lips as he pulled up and pushed down again, shifting position so he was on his knees, sliding closer to Nate's arse.

Nate clutched his arms and voiced his enjoyment. His hips moved again, pumping into Henry's face, speed increasing until he knew Nate was moments away from release. He pulled his mouth off, wrapped his hand firm around his shaft and fisted him until he came.

Pale seed shot high and then flowed over Henry's knuckles. He wiped Nate's seed over his own shaft and head and then he pressed into his lover, using Nate's release to ease the way. His lover's hole slowly widened and he enjoyed the slide, the slow possession of his duke.

He held still above him until Nate opened his eyes. Passion-glazed suited the duke. He waited until his lover met his gaze with more clarity. Henry loved the moment when he was on the brink of thrusting, the moment when he controlled their bliss. For however brief a time the pleasure took, he'd become the duke's master.

He hadn't always been this dominant, this demanding. But escape from the brothel had given him the freedom to choose his lovers. Most often, lovers were taken in darkness with furtive speed. Having Nate's gorgeous body within reach heightened his desire to dominate; and Henry took whatever control he could. He had none other in his life.

When Nate stroked his chest, Henry enjoyed the touch. He tweaked his nipples and adjusted his position so he supported his weight on his hands. Then, he began to move. Thrusting in short jabs until Nate's body relaxed, then lengthening his stroke. Nate's tight ring caressed his whole length and his senses soared. Nate wrapped his long legs loosely around his hips, limiting his stroke but connecting their skin so that each slide brought the most pleasure.

Between them, Nate's cock bobbed, sated. Nate pinched his nipples, twisting both peaks painfully. Henry rose higher; dragging Nate up so only his shoulders remained flat to the bed. Holding him where he wanted him, feet spread wide in the air, Henry slipped in deeper yet. He couldn't breathe, he couldn't stop. He thrust into Nate with everything he had and cried out as desire stole away everything but the feel of Nate's body over his.

Nathan stilled Henry's fidgeting with a hand, readjusting the cravat into place. He'd never dressed anyone before and found the process of covering up his lover as arousing as undressing him. The short carriage ride home would be torture.

"Will you stop fussing?" Henry grumbled and tugged at the unfamiliar knot Nathan had tied.

Sighing, Nathan pushed it back into place. "Leave it be. The carriage should be here and you are far from ready."

"I think the coach is here. Damn."

Nathan admired the man before him. So very, very tempting. Henry turned for the bed, but Nathan caught his arm and pulled him into another kiss. "Until tonight?"

"Nate, we need to be discreet."

Hearing his lover use his given name settled any anxiety Nathan felt. They were together, with no barriers between them. Almost an equal—except for rank and Henry's need to dominate. He could ignore the first and accept the second if it meant happiness could be his at last. "We will muddle through, Henry, never fear." Nathan honestly didn't know how he was going to juggle a lover and a wife under the same roof and hope to avoid detection, but he would not contemplate giving this up.

Henry bit his lower lip. "As you wish, but for God's sake, you need to stop glancing at my groin."

Nathan chuckled. "Forgive me. I'm well aware that good things reside in those trousers and since I'm now allowed to touch it's a bit distracting."

He headed for the door. Before he'd traveled more than a few paces, Henry's hand connected with his rear. Glancing back, Nathan flashed a grin at his bossy servant and fled down the stairs. Brown was waiting.

"Sorry to keep you waiting, Your Grace. A wagon overturned outside the village."

He sighed. "Same excuse as last time. What produce was it today? Pumpkin or turnips?"

Brown had the grace to blush. If he couldn't come up with a better excuse after all these years, he deserved to be called on it. There had been no overturned wagon—it was just an excuse because he'd lingered with a lover. Today Nathan could sympathize with the temptation.

"Mr. Stackpool is waiting for you upstairs. Go and fetch our belongings."

He headed out the front door and climbed into the carriage. Henry joined him a moment later, sitting on the other bench seat, eyebrows drawn together.

Nathan held his peace until the carriage began to move. "What troubles you, Mr. Stackpool?"

Henry sighed and rubbed a hand over his face. "Brown fears there will be trouble awaiting us at Grantley Park. The duchess has been demanding my whereabouts. She has been hinting that I stole her diary."

"I know you didn't and that is all that matters. I promise you, I'll deal with her as soon as possible." Nathan caught Henry's cold hands in his. He met his lover's worry-clouded eyes. If only he could unburden himself about all his marriage problems. Given Henry had suffered to retrieve the diary, he should understand his sacrifice was not in vain. "Someone else wants to embarrass my wife and I. Thanks to the diary I know why but not who. The contents of the diary will actually do more harm to her reputation than to mine. She has been reckless."

"Oh," his lover said slowly, and swallowed.

"Worry not," Nathan murmured. "All will be well soon."

When Nathan could stand his lover's nervous twitching no longer, he tugged his steward across the carriage so they sat side by side. Henry appeared uncomfortable, and to distract him, Nathan fondled his lover's groin.

"We shouldn't . . . not here," Henry whispered, yet drew the blinds over the carriage windows. The vehicle rattled along the rutted road and when they rejoined the main road, Nathan drew the drapes on his windows too.

He quickly opened the fall of Henry's trousers as the carriage gained speed and bent his head. It wasn't, perhaps, the wisest thing to do, yet Nathan couldn't go another minute without feeling his lover close. The thick, full cock popped into view and Nathan licked his lips. He pressed a slow kiss to the head, then opened his mouth wide to take as much in as he could.

Above him, Henry's quick gasp betrayed his pleasure. He grasped Nathan's waistcoat, but Nathan battered his hands away. He would spoil Henry for his hard work and devotion whenever he could, and brought him off quickly.

Henry pulled away first, breathing hard, and looking gorgeously disheveled. He set about putting his trousers to rights and Nathan resumed his seat, cock aching with need. Yet a grim happiness washed over him that he had almost demolished his own handiwork. At least he had another excuse to set Henry's cravat in place again.

CHAPTER ELEVEN

Nathan stepped from the carriage first and glanced at his home. Servants lined the stairs of the sprawling manor house in respectful silence awaiting his every command. He wanted them gone. He wanted to be alone with Henry instead, but he had to behave as he had always done. The servants lined up by seniority, the butler, the valet, flowing down to the lowest pot boy.

He was glad to be back but hated this part coming home.

Considering abandoning the practice, Nathan turned to speak to his butler but then dismissed the idea. As far as he knew they might enjoy the pomp—he'd ask Henry first to gauge the reaction. He glanced back at the carriage as his steward stepped from the dark confines. Someone in the line of servants sighed a hearty relief.

Nathan couldn't agree more. Henry nodded to those gathered but didn't move past Nathan. The formality between them was an irritant that had to be borne. Turning back to the house, Nathan had a brief moment of warning before he was enveloped in a swathe of lily-scented muslin.

The duchess' soft limbs locked around his neck and she hugged him tight. Shocked to the core, Nathan peeled his wife from his arms and thrust her away.

"Oh, Your Grace, I've been so concerned about your absence. You were gone ever so long."

He couldn't decide what he hated more—Sybil's public display of affection or the fact that it was false. "Nonsense, I'm sure you didn't miss me."

Why pretend anymore? She'd taken lovers from among the servants as if they were her due and dismissed them for refusing or when she tired of them. The thought sickened him.

Sybil gripped Nathan's hands and held them tight. "It felt like forever."

Henry stepped around them and headed up the stairs.

"Await me in my study, Mr. Stackpool," Nathan called, tingeing his words with a harsh bite of irritation. He wasn't irritated—just determined not to lose sight of his lover for too long.

Sybil's large eyes grew glassy. "But, I thought you would at least take tea with me?"

Nathan wasn't fooled by that once-endearing expression. He'd learned his lesson. "You know I can't abide tea. I have business to discuss and then I want to see the children."

"They are receiving instruction from their new tutor."

"You've replaced another servant?" He gritted his teeth. The children had actually been enjoying their lessons with him. "What happened with Bridgewater?"

Sybil twitched her sleeve and didn't look him in the eye. "He was impertinent and I dismissed him." She peeked up at him and batted her eyelashes.

More than likely she'd failed to seduce him and lost her temper about it.

"Damn it." Nathan grasped Sybil's arm and hauled her up the stairs. The servants remained in place until they crossed the threshold and then he heard them whispering behind his back. He took his wife into the drawing room and closed the door. "What has come over you?"

She sidled up to him and pressed her hands to his chest. "Am I not allowed to miss my husband?"

He blinked. His wife was flirting with him. Flirting? The woman hadn't done that since their third child had been conceived. "I want to know what Mr. Bridgewater actually did to warrant termination of his employment?"

"He was too familiar with the children."

"In what way?"

"He forgot his place. They need firm guidance at this time in their life not silly games."

What the devil would Sybil know about the children's needs?

Games, when coupled with learning, were an age-old tradition for remembering history. And it was inevitable that a tutor might occasionally slip and speak unguardedly during their lessons. His own tutors had done the same from time to time. It had never affected the strength of their teaching skills. Mr. Bridgewater was an excellent educator. He would have Henry entice him back if he was able.

Thinking of his lover reminded him that Henry might be disturbed by his wife's affectionate greeting and he yearned to reassure the man that nothing had changed. She'd never been one given to amorous displays outside the bedroom, and her greeting on the steps was unprecedented. Nathan moved out of her reach and further into the room, keeping a close eye on her movements.

A seductive smile spread across Sybil's lips as she played with the edge of her gown. "Come, my love, it has been far too long since we have spent any length of time together. Wouldn't you like to spend a little time in my bower? I've missed you."

Hearing Sybil speak as if the past estrangement hadn't occurred unnerved him until a thought slipped into his mind. She was all soft, womanly curves—her face full as if she had eaten more than she should. That couldn't be the case.

Sybil had always been particular about keeping her figure. Even from the time they had first married, she had employed reducing regimes frequently. He feared she had another reason for her pursuit—one that would require his participation to mask.

Instead of anger, he found her predicament amusing.

Perhaps sensing he was softening, she approached him again. Hiding his humor, Nathan ran his hands over her body, cupped her breasts and then slipped them over her belly. He couldn't be sure he felt a new life growing there, but the look on her face, arrested and wary, told him all he needed to know.

She was breeding—and the child certainly wasn't his.

He stepped back. He wouldn't touch his wife again. Sybil had felt all wrong against him. Foreign. "I think I shall go find the children."

Nathan left the drawing room. He didn't glance back but was certain Sybil would be furious. Taking the stairs two at a time, Nathan found the nursery and his children.

Sun-kissed curls greeted him, postures straight as a new-ploughed field. James, Pierce and even little Cecily leaned over slates, writing with all the care they could muster. He stayed quiet, observing his adorable children. Despite having Henry, he'd felt the tug of guilt knowing he'd been away from them.

Showing affection for one's offspring wasn't popular among his set, but he didn't care. They were made in his image. They all had his bright green eyes and his nose.

The new man teaching them looked far too young for the position and far too handsome. He was almost pretty. He didn't know where Sybil might have found him but he could go right back.

Nathan propped himself against the doorframe. "And what mischief have you all gotten into in my absence?"

Excited eyes turned his way, but the children didn't leave their desks. Puzzled, he turned to the tutor and the man hurried to untie them from their chairs. His blood boiled, but he hesitated to react in front of the children. He'd always done his best to shelter them from cruelty. They didn't need to see him slam his fist into their new tutor's face.

When they were free, they ran into his arms and hugged him tight. Pushing aside his rage, he returned each embrace and then set them aside. "Children, who might this person be?"

The children didn't get a chance to reply because the man approached and held out his hand. Nathan looked at it, but didn't take it. "I am Mr. Plumpton, Your Grace. Nephew to your valet. The duchess was kind enough to offer me the position."

Ah, that explained the vague sense of familiarity about his features. "Children, there is a present waiting for you in my study. James, please be sure to share the cause of my delay when you get there. I'll join you all as soon as I can."

James straightened, scowled at the tutor and whisked his younger siblings out the door.

Nathan waited till they were far away then closed the door firmly, shutting away the rest of the house's occupants. "Now then, Mr. Plumpton we need to discuss your employment and continuing good health."

Light footsteps rushed into the study and then the happy squeals of his employer's children assaulted Henry's ears. They didn't give him time to rise from the chair. Cecily burrowed her way past her elder brothers and crawled into Henry's lap. James, the elder, slapped his shoulder a few times, but the middle boy latched around his neck like a barnacle and wouldn't let go.

"Hello children. Pierce, I do need to breathe."

"Come on, Pierce, steady on," James said, tugging on his brother.

The younger boy stepped back, but his eyes were huge. He was afraid. Henry checked the doorway for their father, but the space was empty.

"I'm glad you're back, Henry. It's been dreadfully, frightfully dull without you here," Cecily whispered against his collar. Well, against her father's collar. Henry was still wearing the borrowed suit of clothes.

"Well, I am here now, but I have much to do. Hadn't

you better get back to the nursery? Mr. Bridgewater will be missing you."

"Mr. Bridgewater is gone. Mama dismissed him," Cecily whispered, clinging tighter to his chest.

Henry glanced among the children, but each face agreed. He had often wondered if Bridgewater had been comfortable here at Grantley Park. Donning the guise of a subservient was foreign to Terrance Bridgewater. But this was where they'd agreed to build new lives after the nightmare of the Hunt Club. Henry wished his friend had been given the chance to say goodbye before he'd departed the estate.

Not knowing what to say, he patted Cecily's back and glanced about. Any minute now he expected the duchess to sweep into the room, or at least Nathan to arrive. But given the way the duchess had thrown herself at her husband, he would no doubt be delayed. The thought gnawed at his insides.

Lifting Cecily, he dropped her to her feet. He stood and circled the large desk. There was a wealth of business awaiting his attention. "Either way, you had better return."

"Oh, no, Henry, Papa sent us here to entertain you. He wished to speak to the new tutor."

As relief made him giddy, he tried not to sway into the table. At least Nathan had visited his children before succumbing to his wife's blatant demands for attention and that consideration was sweet music to his soul. To cover his jubilation, Henry picked up the mail, shuffling the invitations that had stacked up: a ball, a dinner, a shooting party, all events that would take Nathan away and exclude him.

Shaking off his sudden black mood, he resolved to make the most of his time with Nathan. Be it in bed or out, every second was worth experiencing.

"I see the children found their present." Nate strode across the room, gaze fixed somewhat lower than it should be.

Shuddering as Nate's obvious desire aroused him, Henry bent to pick up an envelope to hide his physical reaction. That kind of thing had to remain hidden—particularly from the children. They could incriminate them both with an unthinking observation and have them both swinging within a week.

Henry glanced at the children. They deserved a much better treat than him. "A present? They do deserve a treat, don't they?"

Nate frowned, but the children beamed. They bounced in their spots until Henry started counting from one. When he reached three they took position and as one they darted off, searching the room high and low for the candy treats he'd already hidden about the space. Cecily cried out first, and then stuffed the toffee into her mouth. James hollered and hurried to show his father. Pierce was slower, he always was: drawing out the finding so he would have a greater excuse to linger.

Nate frowned. "Henry?"

Henry grinned and touched the side of his nose.

When Pierce swooped on a spot he'd already passed three times, and held up his present for all to see, Nate cheered and rushed to him. It was wonderful to see Nate smile—he did it so rarely.

"Is this how Mr. Stackpool has tricked you into behaving?" Nate laughed. "Hiding my own toffees for a grubby lot of urchins to gobble up? That's outright bribery." He turned, amusement lighting his green eyes to brilliance. "And very clever."

A distraction at the door dimmed Henry's response. The duchess had arrived.

She clapped her hands. "Children, get back upstairs at once. Mr. Plumpton has come at considerable expense to replace that horrid Mr. Bridgewater."

Disappointment trickled through Henry. Terrance had been a wonderful teacher and very patient with the children. Her Grace hadn't liked him because he wouldn't fall into her bed. He couldn't have done anything else to deserve being dismissed.

The children stood stock still and as one turned to their father, a plea clear in every face.

"Mr. Plumpton is dismissed," Nate informed her. "Mr. Stackpool here shall oversee their education until he can persuade Mr. Bridgewater to return."

The duchess turned frosty eyes on Henry, and he considered taking a step back. The venom in her glare hurt even at a distance.

"Children, take Mr. Stackpool on your daily walk, would you? Your mother and I need a few moments."

Dismissed so curtly, Henry heeded little Cecily's tug and left with the children. Once they were clear of the house, the older boy cheered.

"I knew Papa would throw that mean man from the house. I just wish he would have let us watch," James grumbled.

"Now, Master James, your father knows what is best for you."

James dipped his head at the rebuke but then skipped ahead. Pierce chased after.

With Cecily taking such shorter strides, the boys quickly forged ahead on the winding path. When the path curved and they were out of sight of the house, Cecily tugged on Henry's sleeve. He stopped and picked her up.

This was another of their secrets. To keep apace with the boys, Henry had to tote the youngest along in his arms occasionally. He didn't really mind. Cecily was a light little thing and she rarely caused him problems. The duchess, however, would suffer an apoplexy if she found out.

"I really missed you when you were gone," Cecily whispered. "Where did you go?"

Henry hadn't thought to practice an answer suitable for young ears and he floundered. "I, ah, visited with a friend."

"Were they nice?"

Nice was an understatement, but he couldn't wax lyrical about the girl's father. "Yes, I had a very pleasant time."

"Nicer than with me and James and Pierce to keep you company?"

He chuckled. "No, nothing could be that good."

Cecily snuggled into his neck and sighed. "You smell like Papa."

Henry choked. The young girl had always been observant. It was just a matter of time before she noticed his clothes were finer than they should be. He'd have to change soon.

As he walked along, the burden in his arms grew heavier. Cecily fell asleep as he travelled through the woods and when he came to the bubbling stream where the boys had stopped, James hurried to remove his jacket so Henry could put his sister down.

The little girl grumbled, but soon fell still. Henry moved a little away to where the boys stood watching and they both hugged him tight. Moved by the children's affection, Henry returned the embrace.

"We thought you'd gone away for good like the other servants always do," James explained, wiping his eyes with his shirt sleeve, but trying to hide the action from his younger brother.

"Mama said you'd run away." The younger son bit his lip and gazed at Henry with such accusation than he grew embarrassed. He hadn't thought the children would notice his leaving more than with any other servant.

"Well, I had a little time away, but I'm back now and here to stay."

Pierce dug his toe into the earth. "Promise?"

"Yes, I promise." No matter what happened between him and Nate or with Nate and his harpy of a wife, Henry would remain a loyal servant to the family. He only hoped the children never learned the depth of his entanglement with their father.

Appeased, the two boys approached the stream and hunkered down to watch for fish. On a warm day, they liked to wade out and attempt to catch them bare handed. Henry didn't think it a good day to try it and told them so. Given the tension in the house, he had no wish to have the children scolded for any inevitable fall.

Henry smiled at the boys. "What did you three get up to in my absence?" He looked about him, glad to be home. He hadn't counted on missing the place so much, but when the carriage had rumbled through the gates he had known the truth. He was safe. He was home. Noticing the boys hadn't answered, Henry glanced at them. They shifted uneasily and looked at each other. "Come on, out with it. It cannot be all that bad—the manor is still standing."

"We listened."

"Listened?" Henry looked between them and the boys blushed. "To what?"

"Oh, lots of things," James gave up his fish-watching and sank down beside him. He leaned against Henry's shoulder. "Cecily started it."

"Go on."

"She visited Mama's room one night and heard her moaning. She was really worried, but Papa's valet marched her back to bed. Cecily said he was all white and fishlike. He scared her so much that she didn't tell us until the next morning."

Nate's valet had likely bedded the mistress that night. Poor Cecily—to come upon such a scene at her age. Henry hoped she never understood what her mother liked to do with the servants. But it could not be good that the duchess had entertained another in her bed. She was still young enough to deliver a child. Nate would be furious if she grew bellyful with a servant's seed. He hoped nothing came of it. "Did Cecily tell your father?"

"I don't think so. Mama came out and threatened to take away all her dolls if she breathed one word about it. Cecily is exceedingly fond of them, you know."

"Of course." Trust the child to skip over the implications of his mother's infidelity and hone in on the truly important matters: dolls.

"And then I started watching Mama's door, too, when Papa went away. The valet spent each night in mama's bedchamber, but I think he might have hurt her. She called out ever so loudly."

Concern for the child filled him. "Did you go in?"

"No, I was going to, but then I heard her thank him. Does Mama like pain?" James' brow scrunched. "She always claimed she suffered for our births."

Henry scrambled for a way to turn the conversation. "A lot of women say that—especially when their children are troublesome."

James leaned heavily against his shoulder and burrowed. Getting the hint to offer more comfort, Henry lifted his arm and encircled the boy. "Cee Cee didn't sleep much while you were away. I kept her company during the night."

Henry grinned. "You were a very good brother. I'm proud of you."

The older boy yawned and then after a minute or two he slept as well.

Henry looked over at the younger boy, but Pierce was still watching the fish.

As if feeling eyes upon him, Pierce scowled at his brother and sister then shook his head. "No sense, that pair. Night time is for sleeping—not gadding about."

CHAPTER TWELVE

The children returned to the nursery for their evening meal while Henry turned below. The servants' hall was awash with activity, yet when his presence was noted, they all fell silent and hurried to take a seat. Thanks to his position, he'd always garnered respect, especially as he had the duke's ear. If they knew he'd had their master's cock as well that respect would disappear altogether.

Silence was extremely rare in the servants' hall. He stepped through and took his place beside the butler. Henry glanced around, wondering if they knew or suspected. Not too many met his eye.

Unwilling to let the silence unnerve him, he cleared his throat. "I understand Mr. Bridgewater was dismissed in my absence. Would anyone care to inform me if he communicated his plans for future employment? The duke has indicated he'd like him reinstated."

The butler and housekeeper exchanged a long glance. The butler leaned closer. "I am so pleased to hear this. Mr. Bridgewater hasn't departed the estate as yet. I managed to convince him to remain until the duke returned."

Henry let out a relieved breath. "Excellent. Have him report to me in my office tonight. Or perhaps, you had better tell me where he's hiding until I can speak to the duke."

"He's bunked down with the gardeners. Seems as happy as a lark out there, despite the poorer accommodations."

Thank God Terrance was still here. He had to warn

him about Lewes and the location of his country estate. Neither of them had heard of it when they'd sought employment from the Duke of Byworth. They thought themselves free of ties to the past. "Excellent. I'll see him after dinner."

Henry picked up his silver and forced food down his throat. The other servants filled the silence with gossip about the duke and duchess. They were to dine together tonight, they said, the duchess had made extensive plans for the duke's evening.

Unexpected and ridiculous jealousy turned his stomach into knots. He quickly finished his dinner and stepped out of the manor. He didn't want to overhear the servants discuss whether their employers were mooning at each other over the crystal glassware.

He took the winding path through the shrubbery.

Terrance Bridgewater approached in a rush, weaving his way along the path and pulled Henry into his arms. He squeezed tightly. "I thought you'd never get out of there."

"Bloody Hell, Terrance, you stink of the manure pile." He brushed at the sleeves of Nathan's coat furiously.

Terrance chuckled. "Best way to hide from the notice of the great house. Not too many visit the gardener's patch."

Henry held Terrance at arms' length then checked the immediate area for others. He breathed a sigh of relief that they were alone but he would still guard his words. "Two things. Byworth wants you to continue as tutor, but . . . the Duke of Lewes is in the area. Arrow had an unpleasant encounter with him at his country estate. He's looking for Archer."

Understanding widened Terrance's eyes at the mention of their former names. Terrance caught Henry's face and turned him toward the moonlight. He winced at the bruises that still darkened his jaw. "He caught Arrow?"

"Unfortunately, yes. However, he does not know where

the man resides. But Lewes' residence is known to Byworth and he, in fact, saved Arrow. Our employer also knows about the Hunt Club and what goes on there. He's a member but I never saw him. Did you?"

Terrance hissed, and raked a hand through his hair. "No, I did not. So, we leave tonight?"

"No." Henry crossed his arms over his chest. "Byworth will overlook the issue of my employment at the club. He does not now about you. He has similar inclinations to my own."

Terrance whistled. "Never expected that."

Henry shrugged. "Very surprising." Actually, his mind still reeled that the Duke of Byworth desired him the way he did.

"So, does Arrow have a new master?"

Henry scowled. Most times he'd been the submissive partner in any Hunt Club appointments, and Terrance knew that very well. But he wouldn't be anyone's property in the bedroom again.. "No. Arrow retired, if you remember."

Terrance nodded. "So, you are safe here. Thank God."

Henry clutched his friend's shoulder. "You will be too. But you will need to stay out of sight for a while. At least until Lewes leaves the district. I'll do my best to find out when he does."

Terrance offered a wry smile. "Lewes has remarkable persistence. If he found you here and you slipped out of his grasp he will search for you again. What conversation did you have with him? I hope nothing that could lead him to your location."

Henry thought over their conversation, and his stomach dropped to his boots. "I told him I was in service."

"Hell."

Exhaustion tugged at Nathan. As he sat down to dine formally with his wife, he thanked the stars he had servants lining the walls. He suffered no false modesty over his looks. He was handsome and appealed to the ladies, and men with similar inclinations, but he had seriously misjudged his own worth.

Fighting off his wife's attentions all through the long afternoon had tried his patience. She was determined to have him. He should have kept the children close. With their demanding ways, he would never have noticed how often Sybil played with the laced edge of her gown, or the way she fluttered her lashes.

He wanted Henry, not Sybil.

Having his thoughts turned toward pleasure so often reminded him of the hours he'd gone without. Henry didn't tease—he took. Nathan's desires were his to mold, his to release. He was too far gone to return to his old life.

He picked up his cup of claret and took a deep swallow. Sybil hurried to do the same and her smile suggested she hoped he'd keep drinking. Did she think he would be more manageable that way? Nathan didn't oblige her. He drank sparingly, ate well and when the last course was cleared away, he escorted her into the drawing room. "I say, are you not feeling well, my dear?" he asked. "I noticed you ate less than your usual sparrow-like portions."

"I am taking a reducing regime. My appetite will return in due time." Sybil sat and arrayed herself on the chaise lounge. Nathan wasn't fooled—he'd noticed her grimace as roast pork landed on her plate. She'd cut up the strong-scented meat, but pushed it around. Not one bite had crossed her lips.

"You do dabble in nonsense. A reducing regime is hardly necessary." And couldn't be good for a woman who was breeding. During her pregnancies with James, Pierce and Cecily, Nathan had pressured her to eat. The vain fool had been terrified to lose her figure.

"Nathan, darling, it is so wonderful to hear your concern. Do come sit by me." Sybil patted the deep blue cushion next to where she sat, but he shook his head and sat opposite in a wingback chair. He studied her and she had the grace to fidget. Then to his considerable surprise, she stood, walked across the room and settled on his lap. "Must you be so distant?"

"Must you be so familiar? Get off me."

She stumbled away from the irritation in his voice. "You are such a beast."

"I am many things, my dear, but a fool is not one of them. You're breeding."

Sybil stared at him a moment then rushed to the open window and half flung herself out. She heaved up the contents of her stomach and lay limply where she fell.

Unimpressed, Nathan stood and poured a glass of water for her. As he approached his wife, he held out the glass. He might not love her anymore, but he didn't hate her. "Sip it slowly." Hate could come later. Especially if she did anything to publicly embarrass him or the children.

She slid to the floor, but took the glass from his fingers and tasted a dainty sip. Perspiration beaded her skin. Nathan pulled out a handkerchief and patted her brow. Sybil leaned toward him, but he yanked his hand away. He would not be fooled into doing her bidding. She should have taken more care.

"You must hate me," she whispered.

He crossed his arms over his chest. "What I feel is no concern of yours. You made your bed now you must live with the consequences. Your diary proved interesting reading, by the way. Do tell me how the Duke of Lewes came to have it? I do not enjoy being blackmailed by that bastard."

A flurry of tears fell over her cheeks in precise waves. Another of her tricks—Sybil could cry on cue. "I'm so sorry. I'll make it up to you."

There was nothing Sybil could do or say, no amount of blackmail to pay, that would make the Duke of Lewes forget what he'd read in that diary. "Was it worth it?"

More tears fell. "We can flee the scandal. Go somewhere no one knows us and start again."

"What a generous offer you make. Well, you can't start over with me and certainly not when another man's bastard grows fat in your belly." His harsh words made her flinch, a real emotion, he thought.

"Don't say that."

"Why not? It is the truth. I will never acknowledge that child. If you're going to tumble every servant we employ the least you could do is have the man withdraw before he finishes."

"I do not bed every servant."

Nathan heard the distinction she made. "So, not all my employees have cuckolded me. Thank you for that?"

Sybil blushed. "He loves me," she whispered softly.

Nathan stopped laughing immediately. He glanced at Sybil and believed her. She wasn't saying it to hurt him. She used no tricks to mold her words. He stood and stalked the room, his pulse thundering in his veins. Having Sybil declare the love offered by another man should be cause for distress, but it wasn't. He was thinking about Henry again. About the bond of respect and admiration they shared. "You should leave, Sybil."

"No, I cannot leave you. I promised to love and obey you."

Her words pieced his thoughts and settled around his heart. "But I don't love you. Not anymore." He loved Henry—his whole being throbbed with the need to tell his steward this very minute to see if his love was returned.

Sybil sobbed, a mixture of real and fake emotions filling the room. When she lifted her head to stare at him, Nathan felt nothing but peace. He nodded, decision made. "The Rye estate is in good repair and the countryside conveniently pretty. Go there for your confinement. Perhaps the scandal of our divorce won't follow you."

"You mean to set me free?" She gazed at him, disbelief plainly written across her pale face.

Nathan nodded.

His wife licked her lips, stood and shook out her skirts. "I shall need to take some servants with me."

He sat and looked at his properly composed wife, marveling that he had just arranged a separation with so little fuss. "Take as many as you need—but particularly take whoever fathered that child. If I learn who he is and he is still under this roof, I would have to make an example of him."

She swayed but hurried for the door.

"Oh, and Sybil, make sure you are gone before the children rise in the morning. I will use my own words to explain your sudden departure to them."

Nathan didn't believe she would go near them, she never informed them of her sudden departures before, but he would be the one to break the news. She had shown them little love, about as much as she would a pretty bauble. The children deserved better. They needed someone who would play games with them and give them treats. A person who would tuck them in at night.

They deserved Henry.

He stayed in the drawing room brooding about his lover while above him footsteps hurried to and fro. After an hour had passed, the panicked activity lessened and Nathan made his way to his bedchamber. He passed no one: all activity centered in the wing distant from his. Pleased beyond words to find his valet had already retired, Nathan poured another drink and sank into an armchair.

He loved Henry.

With all his body and soul he yearned for the other man. Unsure of how to proceed, Nathan kept drinking until oblivion swallowed him.

Henry woke as little fingers pulled on his hair. He dragged himself upright and blinked into the dark bedchamber.

"Oh, good you're awake." Cecily climbed onto the bed and threw herself into his arms. The little girl's warm embrace tightened.

"What are you doing wandering around?" He stroked down the length of loose blonde curls as unwelcome emotions tugged at him. He couldn't care too much about her or either of the boys. They were not his to love.

"I had a bad dream." Cecily burrowed against his chest and he unwisely pressed his lips to her hair. Try as he might, he couldn't stop the flow of affection he had for this little scamp. She and her brothers deserved as much love as they could get. They got precious little from their mother.

"Well, you're safe now, but you should be back in bed. Go on."

Cecily shook her head. "Will you take me?"

Knowing he had to return her, Henry extracted himself from her grip and slid a robe over his nightshirt. Given Cecily's past erratic nightly visitations, he'd taken to wearing the pesky nightshirt for propriety's sake.

She jumped into his arms and hung on tight. Halfway down the servant's staircase, he heard voices from the lower floor. Curious, but burdened with Cecily, he shrugged off the thought to inquire and concentrated on navigating the stairs.

James and Pierce were deeply asleep, and he tiptoed past them, lowered Cecily to her bed and tucked her in. The little girl pounced on her favorite doll and hugged it tightly. Henry settled on the bed and rubbed her back until her breathing evened. When he was certain she slept, he weaved between the beds, straightening bedclothes around the boys. They didn't stir so much as a muscle.

When he closed the door behind his back, there were even more servants about. Candlelight glowed from the entrance hall and footmen carried luggage out into the night. Was Nate going somewhere?

Heart in his mouth, Henry watched Nate's valet scurry through the front door and then the duchess, cloak pulled over her head, stepped outside. They were leaving. His heart settled like lead in his chest. How could Nate leave without a word?

Gripping the railing tight, he watched the front door close and stared at it long after. The butler blew out candles and retired while Henry listened to the carriage fade into the distance.

Why was he surprised? The duke could do as he wished and had likely slaked his lust, knowing Henry would be here when he returned.

The house grew silent and still, but Henry's heart pounded. Nate hadn't even said goodbye to the children. Had he been so wrong about the man's character?

Afraid that his distress could be observed should someone stumble along the hall, Henry pivoted and returned to his room. Once there, he buried his head in his hands and shook.

CHAPTER THIRTEEN

Nathan sat up on the settee in surprise. Strong sunlight pierced the room, indicating the late hour. Hell's teeth, what a night. Blinking, he looked around and registered the cold hearth, the curious silence, and the absence of his valet.

Usually the meticulous man woke him by eight, laid out clothing and arranged bathwater before escorting a footman in with his breakfast. Nathan liked the routine and relied upon it. Peering at the clock, he was surprised to find it was as late as a quarter past ten.

Damn foolish day to change the schedule. Today marked the first day of his freedom and he had many things to do. But first of all he needed a bath and a change of clothing. Then he wanted to see his children and explain their mother's departure.

Running explanations through his mind, Nathan stood and pulled the bell. He was also anxious to see Henry. After days of close contact, the separation of a few hours was agony. He missed waking next to him, although his steward might not have enjoyed sleeping on the settee as Nathan had done last night. Henry belonged in a bed, with luxury and every comfort he could offer.

Nathan stood and stretched. He was getting too old to fall asleep just anywhere. He wanted to wake up in his bed. He wanted Henry to rouse him with kisses, but he had to endure his valet's stark efficiency, not the comfort of a lover's touch. They could only manage that at the cottage.

When the valet didn't answer his summons promptly, he scowled at the door to his dressing closet. It was unlike the valet not to arrive when called, so he stalked to the room and through to his valet's connecting bedchamber. The room was empty. Irritated anew, Nathan stalked back to the racks of clothes and considered his choices. His valet was neat to a fault. Country, evening, London splendor—he just had to choose the occasion.

A few minutes later, after he'd selected a somber green to mark his wife's departure, the door to his bedchamber creaked open.

"Where the devil have you been? It's well past . . ."

"May I be of service, Your Grace?"

Nathan looked up as the unexpected voice interrupted his rant. The butler returned his gaze, a bright flush brightening his features.

"Where the hell is . . . ?" Nathan didn't finish as his sluggish brain connected the changes of last night with his late awakening and the butler's obvious embarrassment. His valet had left with his wife. Nathan swung away from his servant. Of course, the sneaky bastard. There was no way Nathan would give that man a letter of recommendation when he left his service. Hell, he could leave it now. He refused to pay the man who fathered his wife's bastard child.

Nathan glanced out the window, fighting the urge to reach over and throw something. It was one thing for his wife to cuckold him, another for a servant, and a personal one at that, to be a party to the mess. The servants would be sniggering behind his back. By his outburst, the butler would know that Nathan hadn't a clue about his wife's treachery.

Behind him, the butler cleared his throat, reminding him he had company. Without turning to see the pity in his servant's eyes, Nathan spoke. "Bath, breakfast, and Henry. In that order."

He needed to cool his head before he faced his lover.

"Henry, Your Grace?"

Nathan shut his eyes. Of all the stupid slips. Henry wasn't known by his given name, not to anyone but him. He'd have to exercise more care. He ground his teeth. "Mr. Stackpool."

"Oh, yes, of course." The butler hurried off, leaving Nathan alone with his ill temper. Right under his nose the whole time. How could he have been such a fool?

The door opened and closed behind his back, but Nathan didn't turn. Not even when the fast footsteps paused behind his back and a breath whispered across his neck.

"You stayed?"

Nathan turned, catching the dazzling smile on Henry's face. He had never known him to appear so happy. He frowned. "Where else would I be?"

Henry linked his hands together across his belly and Nathan covered them. He couldn't do any more. Any minute now, servants would arrive with pails of water, but he had to connect with his lover. Had to touch him, feel the heat of his strong hands. Had to know that this odd love he believed was reciprocated.

"Your wife left last night." Henry cocked his head to one side and his smile dimmed.

"That she did. She couldn't possibly stay. Henry, I need to add to your duties. I'll need you to fill in as my valet."

Henry glanced around. "What happened to Jones?"

"He ran away with his one true love."

The other man scoffed. "It's not possible for him to run away with himself. He must be cleverer than he looks."

Nathan smiled at Henry's absurd observation. "Smarter than I am, at any rate."

Henry clucked his tongue. "It is a pity Her Grace has already departed. She has strong opinions about the correct demeanor for the position of valet. She could have found a replacement on her travels. The lady is so particular about your clothes."

"The duchess has requirements in a valet that exceed my desires." Nathan brushed his hand across Henry's sleeve.

Henry eased back. "Has the duchess gone to London?"

"No, she ran off with her one true love too."

Watching Henry try to puzzle out his words erased his anger. Neither he nor his wife had loved each other enough not to turn to another. Sybil could have his valet, and Nathan would keep his steward. He walked his fingers up Henry's waistcoat and adjusted his cravat. When it was perfect, he caressed his lover's cheek.

There was so much about this man to love. Loyalty, strength and above all else, very kissable lips. The man's body was very distracting. Nathan leaned in and kissed Henry's plump lower lip.

Henry's eyes widened. "He. They. Oh, good God."

"Far more eloquently expressed than my poor attempt." Nathan leaned in and kissed Henry full on the mouth. Hunger beat against his senses as their tongues tangled, but footsteps in the hall drew closer and they parted.

While the footmen lingered filling the bath, Nathan kept his gaze on the view outside his windows. His cock subsided swiftly, but he didn't want to take a risk. His heady lust for Henry had killed his anger as if it had never been. Behind his back, Henry directed the servants. When the bath was filled and breakfast laid out, his steward dismissed them.

With Henry filling in as his valet, Nathan could justify moving his lover to this floor. After a thorough cleaning, he could take up residence in the room adjoining Nathan's dressing closet. They would have complete privacy.

Nathan heard the click of the lock and turned. He stood still as Henry stalked toward him. His desire for the other man surged back to life and with it his cock thickened. But he didn't get the kiss he wanted.

Henry circled and then pushed at his back. "Strip and have your bath."

Thrilled to carry out the order, Nathan quickly did as he was told, lingered beside the bath in the hope of receiving a slap for tardiness. When he got nothing for his disobedience, he stepped in. Warm water coated his balls, but his erection remained.

Behind him, china clinked and then Henry came forward carrying a teacup.

He snorted. "I've never eaten breakfast in the bath before."

"Nathan, I am currently reassessing what you may not have done. But I would wager you have tried most things."

"I tried you." Nathan grinned. "I definitely liked you."

Henry turned away but came back with a chair, sitting it close to the bath. He leaned forward and took the teacup before Nathan finished. "Only liked?"

Their eyes met and held. Henry finished Nathan's tea and settled back with his knees slightly apart. Nathan almost crawled out of the bath. "Well." He washed his balls while he stalled for time. How did one confess to another man that they were loved? "Perhaps, more than that. A great deal more in fact."

His steward's usually placid face split into a blindingly happy smile. He stood, ruffled Nathan's hair and headed to the table to replace the empty teacup with a heaped plate of food. When he returned, Henry's smile had dimmed somewhat, yet there was a peace about him that made Nathan's heart pound fast.

Desire surrounded them, curling into his belly and banished any thought of eating. Settling the offered plate to the floor, Nathan poured water over his head and scrubbed his hair. Henry hadn't said a word. Nothing but a smile.

"Are you clean yet?"

Certain he'd scrubbed enough, Nathan stood, toweling

himself dry without a word. Was that it? Was that all the reaction he could expect to his admission? Nathan glanced at his lover. While he had been busy drying himself, Henry had rearranged the room. He sat on a straight backed chair but another was placed facing it. Puzzled, he approached and dropped his towel on the opposite chair.

"Don't speak," Henry said, his voice lowered so it wouldn't carry. "And make sure to keep your enjoyment as quiet as you can. We don't want to be disturbed, do we?"

Forbidden to speak, Nathan shook his head. Henry turned him so when he stopped, he faced a padded chair.

Henry's lips brushed Nathan's ear. "Put your hands on the seat."

Bending at the waist, he touched the chair, but Henry's hand settled on his spine and flattened his back so he was angled from the hips instead. His bottom rocked back toward the other chair. He blushed as Henry's warm hands coasted along his sides, stroked over the curve of his rear and settled on his hips. Henry tugged and Nathan took a step back, but kept his hands on the chair.

His breath caressed Nathan's buttocks sending delicious shocks to his cock. A chair creaked and Henry tightened his grip on Nathan's thighs. His legs were forced apart. Without permission to speak, without the ability to moan, Nathan gritted his teeth and glanced down. Henry's feet stretched forward, knees resting inside his and holding his thighs wide.

Warmth pressed to his left cheek and Nathan took in a steadying breath as pleasure tightened his balls. Henry kissed the whole of his left cheek, and then switched to the right. By the time he'd covered the right in kisses, Nathan was desperate to moan.

Henry began to knead the muscles of his thighs. Erotic and compelling, they slid over his bare skin, dimming his hunger somewhat. Lips returned, deliciously wet against his lower back. Fingers stroked up over his buttocks and then Henry's thumbs slowly opened Nathan's arse. His breath brushed his hole and Nathan gripped the chair tighter. Henry pressed his lips firmly there and then his tongue licked. He went up on his toes.

He'd never had this done to him.

His lover slung his arm over Nathan's lower back, holding him down flat on his feet. The other fingers spread his cheeks wider and then his lips returned, kissing then licking across his entrance, filling Nathan with so much hunger that he closed his eyes.

Henry lavished so much attention there that Nathan rocked back into his face. Firm hands pulled his arse cheeks open wide. Henry groaned then stabbed his tongue into Nathan's hole.

Sweet merciful heaven. He was going to spend. Fluid seeped in a long string from his cock as his arse was stuffed full. God, he loved everything Henry did to him. The man was full of surprises. Stubble scratched across his cheek and those talented lips worked down to torture his balls. A moan escaped him.

Henry slurped back up to his arse again and this time his penetration was harder, furiously demanding entry to Nathan's body. The chair under his fingers creaked as he held back his release. He would have succeeded had Henry not pressed his tongue deep and slipped his hand over Nathan's cock. Pleasure boiled out in waves, coating the towel covered chair with strings of fluid.

Near to sobbing, Nathan didn't realize that Henry had moved until the blunt head of his cock started pressing inside him. He gasped, struggling to accept the hard length invading. He widened his stance, relaxing into Henry's possession.

Taking the other man deep stung at first, but his lover was patient, letting Nathan adjust to his size before he began to thrust. Henry ran his hands over Nathan until he wriggled back, taking more and encouraging his lover to move.

Henry didn't oblige. He curled his arms around Nathan and held them tight together. "So incredibly perfect. How did I get this lucky?"

Nathan's breath caught. Impaled by hard length, he couldn't shift to see his lover's face. Henry pulled back, and then thrust. His powerful movements and the words stirred Nathan's desire.

With quick demanding thrusts, he had Nathan's pleasure at the brink again. He pounded hard, and Nathan braced himself against the chair to keep his balance. Arse burning, cock slapping against his belly, he ground his teeth. He wanted the release to be sweet; he wanted them to spend together.

Henry changed the angle, fingers digging into Nathan's shoulders and aligning their bodies for a better fit. Coarse hair brushed his inner thighs and their balls slapped together.

Nathan grabbed blindly for the chair to retain their balance as Henry lifted him to his toes.

"You can spend now, Nate."

Pleasure spiked and flowed at the words. Heat flooded Nathan's arse as Henry spent with huge thrusts, biting down on Nathan's shoulder to muffle his groan.

As the tremors lessened, Henry kept moving, working his release until fluid began to slide down Nathan's thighs. Breathing hard, Nathan reached over his shoulder to keep his lover close. He tightened his fingers in Henry's sweat-dampened hair. "I love you."

Henry withdrew, and turned Nathan to face him. Bright eyes smiled back at him. Nathan seized his lover's head and dragged him close for a kiss.

But Henry pushed him away. "You need a bath. I dirtied you."

"So you did and I liked it." His heart filled with love for the other man. "When I'm dressed I must speak to the children about their mother's departure."

Henry gave him another nudge in the direction of his bath. "Of course, shall I await you downstairs?"

"No, we should see them together." He sighed. "I plan to divorce her Henry and I may need your help in making them understand it's nothing to do with them."

His lover's eyes widened. "Are you sure that's the right thing to do."

"I am." He winced, dreading what was to come but longing for it just the same. "I think she wants her freedom as much as I do. I want no secrets between us, Henry. I will undoubtedly need your help and good sense very much in the coming months. I just want you to know that the past three years, because of your presence, has made such a difference to my life. To the children's lives, too. We are all happier with you around and I would hate you to feel unequal simply because I pay you a wage. You are so much more to me than that."

Although Henry's eyes widened with the admission, his lover nodded. It didn't make him a lesser man to admit he needed help. He was smart enough to know he'd need Henry for the rest of his life.

While he was imagining a wonderfully decadent future, Henry swept Nathan into his arms and, to his considerable shock, dumped Nathan into his cold bath, splashing water everywhere.

Nathan spluttered and wiped water from his eyes. "You do realize you have to clean that mess up, don't you, sir?"

Henry leaned close over him. "Of course, Your Grace, I live to serve."

Nathan threw his head back and howled with laughter.

EPILOGUE

"The Duke of Lewes and Duke of Staines," Nathan's butler intoned.

He risked a quick glance at Henry before standing to greet his guests. His lover appeared nervous. "Gentlemen, what an unexpected surprise."

The Duke of Staines, flanked by his ever-present footman, stalked across the room and pulled Nathan into a rough hug. Nathan's first lover set him at arm's length and grinned. "I got your note and decided to pay our mutual friend a visit. I believe he has seen the error of his ways."

Lewes, dark shadows beneath his eyes standing stark against his pale skin, grimaced as he drew closer. "Byworth."

Nathan crossed his arms over his chest and stared the man down.

"Nate!" Staines snapped. "Enough. He's been suitably punished for his actions I promise you."

Yet while Lewes should have enjoyed that immensely, he didn't appear content. His gaze darted about the chamber and settled on where Henry stood silently behind Nathan.

Staines peered around Nathan too. "Ah, Arrow," he drawled. "I wondered where you'd gotten to. We need to have a little chat."

Henry, or Arrow as he was apparently known in the Hunt Club, didn't flinch from Staines' words but there was no way Nathan would allow his man to go anywhere with them. When Staines glanced at his servant, the groom took a pace toward Henry.

Nathan stepped between. "Leave him be."

The servant, a strapping Irishman Nathan remembered well for his devotion to his duke, hesitated. He cast a questioning glance at his master as Staines approached.

"Nate? Have you formed an attachment to my employee?"

Nathan smoothly kept between Henry and the other men. "Stackpool is my employee. My man, now."

Behind him, Henry growled.

"Touching, don't you think, Redding? Shall we let the lovers remain in peace?" The duke turned to regard his own servant steadily. Redding cocked his head, gaze skimming over Henry with an avid light.

The duke frowned and Redding's gaze returned to his master. "Let it go. He'd only run away again."

Staines nodded and adjusted his sleeve. "Quite right, quite right. To return him to the Hunt Club would only breed dissent. He and Archer caused us trouble enough." The Duke of Staines fixed his gaze on the Duke of Lewes, where he fidgeted. "Arrow, or should I say Stackpool, where is Archer?"

Nathan tucked a hand behind his back and motioned for his steward to come closer.

Henry grasped Nathan's hand tight. "I don't know, Your Grace. We became separated shortly after we left the club."

Although Staines smiled at his and Henry's new proximity, Nathan couldn't care less. He had to do something to show Henry his support. He'd shoot his former lover if he made an attempt to drag Henry back to a life as a whore.

"How did you leave London?"

Henry squeezed Nathan's hand tighter. "I took the stage."

"Ah," Staines shifted to stand before Nathan. "I'm curious now, indeed. Where did you met Arrow, Nate? You might be a member but you've never patronized the Hunt Club's whores to my knowledge."

As he came closer, Nathan moved back. "He presented

himself to me here."

Staines leaned into him and pressed his lips to Nathan's. The kiss, an intimacy they hadn't shared in years, surprised him. "Liar," Staines whispered against Nathan's lips. "You hired him in London. I remember you telling me you'd found a new steward over drinks at the club. It appears to me your loyalties have shifted, Nate."

His heart pounded. "They have."

The duke's smile was bittersweet, the bright light dimmed from his eyes. He turned to his servant. "Tossed aside again, Redding. Come, let's drag my world-weary heart back to London. Perhaps some new diversion will present itself."

With that, the Duke of Staines left the chamber. Only Lewes remained.

Lewes, however, appeared uncertain for the first time since Nathan had known him. He licked his lips, tossed back his shoulders and approached. "I want to find Archer. Will you help me?"

Henry's hand grew clammy in Nathan's and he tightened his grip on his steward. "From what I've heard, what you want from this Archer is so bad he fled from you. Why should we help do anything after what you put Henry through?"

"I am sorry." Lewes raked a hand through his hair, and tugged. "I know you'll never believe me, not after my recent behavior, but I must have him back. I . . . I need him. I'll die without him."

From behind Nathan's back, Henry hissed, "He'll die by your own hands if he comes back to you."

Nathan pulled Henry close, standing bodily between Lewes' temper and his lover.

Lewes shook his head and didn't meet their gaze. "A mistake I will never make again. I promise you, Arrow. Where is he?"

"Hiding from you. You won't find him. And he won't come back to you of his own free will."

Lewes' expression grew pained. "Dammit, can you get word to him?"

"Perhaps," Henry conceded.

Lewes' jaw clenched, then he bit out, "Can you send something to him?"

"Maybe."

Lewes fussed with his clothes and withdrew a small key. His hand shook as he passed it to Nathan. "The key belongs in my London residence. Will you give that to Archer?"

Nathan snorted. "You're giving him a house key."

Lewes, however, gulped as the key passed into Henry's safekeeping. "No, it doesn't open the house, but it does open something more valuable to me. Tell him I give it of my own free will. He will know to what you refer." He swallowed nervously, nodded and departed.

Behind him, Henry let out a relieved breath and bent his head to Nathan's shoulder.

He pressed his head against Henry's. "Any ideas what the key is for?"

"Perhaps."

Nathan spun. He'd had enough secrets to last a lifetime and wouldn't stand for them any longer. "You know, I'm starting to dislike that word on your lips. You say it too damn much. You do know where this Archer is, don't you?"

"My apologies, Your Grace. Some secrets are not mine to tell." His gaze turned curious. "Is there something else I should be saying? Surely the location of the man Lewes wants isn't that important to you. You seem suddenly ill tempered."

He threw his hands up in despair. "Well, of course there is. I've unburdened myself to you, and to my oldest acquaintances just now. Surely I am not alone with my feelings."

Henry grinned suddenly, stepped forward into the circle of Nathan's arms. "I heard you, Nate. I've heard those words spoken too often in my life to place much store in their value. You would be amazed at how often men and women boast of love during their pleasure or in the wake of some fit of temper. But if the sun stopped shining tomorrow, and you were gone from my life, I don't think I would continue living without you."

Nathan blinked. In the face of such a statement, words of love were meaningless. He'd have Henry in his life until his dying breath. Just because Henry couldn't say the words, didn't mean Nathan couldn't repeat them often. With time, and persistence, Henry would come to believe them as a truth.

He cupped his lover's skull. "I love you, Henry or Arrow, or whatever the hell your name is. You'll never get free of me, but if it should happen that I leave you first I will wait for you to catch up."

With that, he pulled his servant into his arms and squeezed. Henry's soft chuckle skimmed his ear and Nathan claimed his mouth hungrily, impatient for the privacy of the night to come.

THE END

ABOUT THE AUTHOR

Bestselling historical author Heather Boyd believes every character she creates deserves their own happily-ever-after, no matter how much trouble she puts them through. With that goal in mind, she weaves sizzling English set love stories that push the boundaries of regency era propriety to keep readers enthralled until the wee hours of the morning. Brimming with new ideas, she frequently wishes she could type as fast as she conjures new storylines. While writing full time north of Sydney, Australia, Heather collects dust bunnies in all corners of the house and does her best to wrangle her testosterone-fuelled family into submission.

For more information visit
www.heather-boyd.com

ALSO BY HEATHER BOYD

The Distinguished Rogues Series:
Chills
Broken
Charity
An Accidental Affair
Keepsake
An Improper Proposal
Reason to Wed
The Trouble with Love
Married by Moonlight

The Wild Randalls Series:
Engaging the Enemy
Forsaking the Prize
Guarding the Spoils
Hunting the Hero

Miss Mayhem Series:
Miss Watson's First Scandal
Miss George's Second Chance
Miss Radley's Third Dare

Short Stories:
One Wicked Night
Wicked Mourning
In the Widow's Bed
Love Me Tender
Love Me True
The Almack's Alternative
A Husband for Mary

THE HUNT CLUB SERIES

BARELY A MASTER

The trappings of wealth and power give Aiden Banks, Duke of Lewes, little joy and certainly no pleasure. Tormented by grave mistakes he made in the past, he's learned control of his temper at great personal cost, finally shouldering the blame that he has lost the only man he had ever loved through his own actions. His only remaining goal is to educate his young heir to take his place as duke and then he will be free of his responsibilities.

Terrance Bridgewater has freedom at long last with no one to slow down his pursuit of reckless adventure. In London briefly en route to a ship bound for the continent, brings him face to face with his past. Running into the dark and dangerous Duke of Lewes is a complication he'd hoped to avoid. Despite his mistrust, the volatile duke's plea for a second chance tempts Terrance to lower his guard but on his terms only. Yet what can come of two souls with nothing in common but lies, opposing desires, and with far different futures ahead?

HARDLY A STRANGER

The Duke of Staines has the worst luck in wives and lovers. A widow for fifteen years, Ambrose is busy running his gentleman's club, snatches pleasure from transient lovers, and relies on Francis Redding to provide intelligent companionship between social engagements. There is only one problem with his relationship with Redding; the man would make the perfect lover, if only he wasn't a dependant servant.

Life-long footman to the Duke of Staines, Francis Redding, is hardly a stranger to the disappointment of unreachable dreams or the duke's unorthodox love life. He's lived in the duke's shadow for most of his life, trained as a surgeon at his request, too, and has all too frequently kept the duke out of trouble. It's not a bad life for a farmer's son, until the duke's luck runs out.

On the surface, Raphael has everything he needs: good friends, a title, and membership to the decadent Hunt Club where forbidden pleasure can be had at a moments notice. Pretending is not what he wants. Expectations by family and friends keep his feelings for Lord Claymore at bay. When his best friend returns to London in a black mood, Rafe sets out to cheer him up and make Claymore's upcoming birthday an event to remember.

Shaken and uneasy of his growing attraction to men, James has reached an uncomfortable crossroads in his well-ordered, respectable life. Plans to end his torment on his birthday are mere days away. However, his intention to explore forbidden passion just once comes unstuck. Can James follow through with his well-reasoned, sensible decision when a man who knows what he wants, needs him too?

Victor Knight has never been able to juggle his work and love life to anyone's satisfaction. A hardworking investment banker in London, he's obsessed with maintaining his clients' privacy and profits, and cannot understand why those same clients are withdrawing funds when he's making them a good profit. When a dull evening supper at the Hunt Club ends in a blunt invitation to have sex with the Earl of Beecroft, he welcomes the distraction on the proviso they never discuss his business affairs.

Daniel Wellham, the Earl of Beecroft, has long admired Victor Knight. He even understands and admires the banker's preoccupation with work. Their night together is everything he hoped it would be and while he longs for permanence, his secret life as a spy means he can never reveal too much of his own history. Unfortunately, when he realizes that all is not right in Victor's life, those promises he made to keep his nose out of the banker's business means he cannot offer to help or explain that his latest mission might take him away forever. How can love and trust be possible when duty and responsibility prevent total honesty?

www.ingramcontent.com/pod-product-compliance
Lightning Source LLC
Chambersburg PA
CBHW030646190726
48286CB00008B/2686